Principles of American Nuclear Chemistry: A Novel

THOMAS McMAHON

Principles of American Nuclear Chemistry: A Novel

An Atlantic Monthly Press Book
BOSTON · Little, Brown and Company · TORONTO

LIBRARY OF CONGRESS CATALOG CARD NO. 73–117030

01116 39 N2

SECOND PRINTING

The odor amplifier which appears in Chapter 23 is actually another
of the wonderful inventions of Dr. Bernard Vonnegut, who reminds the
author that the mercury adsorption experiments of Agnes Pockels
(1891) preceded and inspired his work.

ATLANTIC–LITTLE, BROWN BOOKS
ARE PUBLISHED BY
LITTLE, BROWN AND COMPANY
IN ASSOCIATION WITH
THE ATLANTIC MONTHLY PRESS

Published simultaneously in Canada
by Little, Brown & Company (Canada) Limited

PRINTED IN THE UNITED STATES OF AMERICA

For Theodore Morrison

Principles of American
Nuclear Chemistry:
A Novel

chapter one

"ARE WE GOING TO SCUFFLE?" my mother was asking my
father. They were supposed to be undressing for bed, but were
wasting time at it. My father was seated on the bed, tuning the
radio.

"If we were Timmy's age, we could fight with our fists.
Wouldn't that be better? We could call each other names."
My mother was removing her earrings. They went into a box
that was too deep and wide to hold them properly. She didn't
have my father's attention. She was slurring her words, difficult to listen to. She was drunk.

"I'd love to hit you," she said.

The three windows of their bedroom looked down from the
third floor into a street that was beginning to be thick with
snow. One of the window sashes let itself be pushed, even bullied, by unseen forces from outside. My mother put something
in her mouth from a tray left over from the party just ended
— glasses on the tray, and cheese, liver paste, crackers, ice,
and herring. In the winter of 1942–43, as this happens, my

3

mother was in her early thirties, pregnant with my younger sister, and uneasy.

She left the room with the tray and returned a minute later without it. But with tears.

"Why did you tell me I was drunk? How did it help anything?"

My father turned off the radio and stood up. He had to turn his back to her to walk to his dresser, but he did. And emptied the change out from his pockets. And took off his tie. "Because when the mother is drunk," he said, "the baby is drunk."

"And this matters to you?"

"Yes," my father said.

"Why?"

But this was the last word she would get out of him. They put out the lights and the snow piled up on Commonwealth Avenue outside. The storm was ending by becoming mixed with freezing rain. Snowstorms always did that in Boston as the winter was establishing itself: it was something the ocean caused.

"Because you're a prude," my mother said, from her side of the bed. "Just like all your friends are prudes." Perhaps, in reviewing their faces, she reconsidered characterizing them as my father's friends exclusively. "Our friends," she said. "I should be sorry to give them a farewell party. I should be sorry to see them go. But I'm not."

The furniture was that same dormitory furniture everybody has to have when they're graduate students. My parents still had theirs, although my father was working as an assistant professor at MIT by the time this was going on. The set of dressers came from the Saint Vincent de Paul Society for ten dollars. The bed from a room in my mother's parents' house.

4

Old crayon drawings of mine papered a wall, and the bottom edges of these, stroked from below by overtures from a radiator painted luminous silver, curled and clicked against each other. The floor, a closely joined hardwood which had been expensive in its day, could have used a refinishing if there had not been a war.

"At least they're gone," my mother said. "To wherever it is. And if it's the same as it was with the Sandemans and the Ferrinis, we won't see them again."

The radiator went on stacking layers of heat in the airy spaces above my parents' heads, as if it had a purpose. Perhaps it was constructing an indoor mirage. My mother turned onto her back and spoke to the ceiling: "There was something I wanted to ask you when everyone was gone, but then you had to tell me how I was offending you with my three glasses of beer. I wanted to ask you what they're going to do about their children. From what I could get out of Gloria, they're not going anywhere I would consider bringing children. Where would they go to school? I think it's stupid."

"Gloria doesn't know anything about it," my father said.

"And you do?"

"No, I don't either."

"Well, we can find out all about it after the war," my mother said, "if they can tell us about it then. I'm perfectly happy to let them drop off the edge of the world, if that's what they want to do."

My father wound his watch and joined my mother in bed. "What if we had to go with them?" he asked.

A long silence.

"I hope that's a hypothetical question."

"What if it isn't?"

"Is that true? Have you been asked to go?"

"No," my father said, "but Nachtigall has let me know that I will be asked."

"What are you going to tell them?"

"I don't know," my father said.

Everyone knows it is a mistake to go to bed angry but even more of a mistake to confront someone there with a surprise. There is always this pact: I'll get into bed with you on the condition that you won't surprise me.

"If you go," my mother said, "you go alone."

"Charming."

"Well, what am I supposed to say? I couldn't travel anywhere now if I wanted to. And I'm not having my baby in a lumber camp."

"I'm not suggesting that you do. If I'm invited to join the project, and if I accept the invitation, you would join me after the baby was born."

"If I join you at all."

"Yes, if you join me at all."

"And where's Timmy all this time?"

"He's with you, or with me. I would prefer he stayed with you for as long as possible. Although if I join the project during this summer, it might be best to have him with me then, so that he could start school in the new place with the other children. In any case, if he's with me, he does what the other project children do. I suggest we wait until the invitation is either made or it isn't. Then, if there's a choice about what happens to Timmy for a period of months, we might make it his choice."

The MacLaurins waited in bed. Waited for what? A resolution.

"If they ask you," my mother said, "you could say no."

"I could," my father answered, "but I won't."

6

In considering what was so obviously the promise of an invitation, my father must have felt pleased. It could be understood as a prize, and in fact there was no harm in understanding it so. Ferrini, Orr, Meisner, Sandeman, Ornberg, Zimas: luminous names in nuclear physics, and he knew they were all involved in the project already.

His specific interest had always been thermodynamics, and even at his present age of thirty-six it was possible for him to look into the future and see that no matter how the tides of international purpose or personal accident might sweep him, his first allegiance would always be to the science of Boyle and Carnot, which he had first proved to himself by examples from the clouds and water on his father's Canadian farm. The cool gases of the atmosphere and their laws, the hot gases of internal combustion engines and their same laws, white winter ice and the same laws again — all seemed evidence of a generality between substances which is somehow paradoxical in cities but not on farms.

His parents and sisters had regarded as natural enough his effort to earn a first degree from the University of British Columbia, but misunderstood his wish to go to graduate school at Berkeley and then MIT. Their impression that he was consciously forsaking the farm was in fact the reverse of his real progress, which was ever toward knowing it better. At Berkeley he had his first experience with the new science of quantum mechanics in an introductory course given by a young man named Sandeman, who made it all seem extraordinarily attractive. Sandeman extended his friendship to all of his students, covering them with a great sweeping stroke of it as if this represented an economy over dabbing at each of them individually. Sandeman, son of a New York doctor and graduate of several excellent schools, lavished hospitality on his

7

students for very little other reason than that it made him happy to teach them.

But quantum mechanics, involved as many young sciences are with baroque philosophies and theories for which there are no experiments, revealed itself as only a noble distraction for MacLaurin, who was dedicated to understanding atoms and molecules for their collective motions rather than their individual ones. Certain circumstances led him to MIT and other ones to the roof of his Cambridge apartment building on hot nights, where he often met the three girls who shared the apartment below his. None of these girls was particularly striking in appearance, but all of them possessed some specific attractiveness which led him to take each one as his girl friend serially over a period of two years. The last girl, who played the piano and had a farm background somewhat like his own — if you substitute the plains of Kansas for the plains of northwestern Canada — became his wife in the year he finished his Ph.D. The earliest period of their marriage saw them living in something like a commune shared by not only them but Nelson Nachtigall, once my father's roommate, and other nameless transients. They all shopped together on Saturday in the market district in Boston's North End, and in the winter they played hockey in the street without ice skates.

My father had stayed on at MIT after taking his degree. He had been flattered into doing this by someone who had wanted him to apply the results of his doctoral research to a related problem. A fruitless year passed before he began to understand that his sponsor was assigning direction to his research on the basis of departmental politics. Still, he pressed on and eventually was able to bring something out of what ended up being a long effort. Further projects followed, some of them more successful than others.

8

My father, lying on his back in the darkness, compared the tiresome idiom he had grown into with the new possibility he felt might now be emerging. His present work was leading to things not precise, only pedantic. The people he was collaborating with appeared to be more absorbed in eating their lunches and drinking coffee than in their tasks in the lab. You could expect to work with them every day for five years, watching them unwrap chicken wings and hearing how their children were growing up — but one day the work would be published and you could take up something new. Years later you would meet one of these people, as likely as not still engaged in the same kind of project, and after five minutes' conversation discover, pathetically, that he was actually nostalgic about the time you spent together. Nostalgic about plainness.

And here was something different.

chapter two

FROM MY FATHER'S FILES:

PROCEEDINGS

of the
Third Metallurgical Projects Seminar, 3/1/43

Room 6–122
Massachusetts Institute of Technology

Participants: E. Orr, E. Ferrini, H. MacLaurin, N. Nachtigall, K. Zimas, W. Ornberg, A. Calder, Chairman

A. Calder: Introductions. Here we all are again. If not enough for a quorum, at least enough for an argument. Questions before the meeting starts?

E. Ferrini: What is MacLaurin doing here?

A. Calder: You may know Dr. MacLaurin for his work in gas dynamics. Interested in hypersonic solutions of gas dynamic equations with heat addition; point explosion models. While the rest of us here are atomic physicists, we may soon need Dr. MacLaurin's services for special problems.

E. Ferrini: Only kidding. Glad to have him.

W. Ornberg: Has anyone matches?

A. Calder: Useful to bring each other up to date on mutual problems. Could each give short résumé of current work, with background explanations and brief history where relevant?

N. Nachtigall: What the hell for? Let's tell Harold the punch line now. We have possible superbomb.

A. Calder: Makes more sense to start at the beginning. He can't appreciate how "possible" our superbomb is until he knows details. The whole thing may be wishful thinking. Even if *our* problems in nuclear chemistry were solved, gadget may fizzle because of *his* problems in keeping the reactants together. Would Zimas start?

K. Zimas: 1932, Chadwick discovers neutron at Cambridge. Repeated Bethe and Becker experiment, bombarded beryllium plate with alpha particles. Found new radiation, which he named neutrons, knocks protons out of a block of paraffin with very high energy. Same effect observed with other materials.

N. Nachtigall: Get to the point. BANGO!

A. Calder: Nelse, I've told you why we're going through this.

K. Zimas: The fact that neutrons knock protons out of other materials means they're not gamma radiation.

E. Ferrini: 1934, I shot proton into U-238 nucleus, expecting to find element 93, got element 94 plus four others. Couldn't figure it out.

A. Calder: 1938, Pact of Munich. At Kaiser Wilhelm Institute in Berlin, Hahn, Strassmann, Selina Meisner did Ferrini experiment, tried to separate radium since products are radioactive. Found barium will not separate from the radium. Selina forced to leave Germany as non-Aryan. Went to Orr's lab in Copenhagen.

E. Orr: At my lab, Selina told me she thought Hahn and Strassmann split nucleus without knowing it.

N. Nachtigall: Selina had a little BANG for herself.

A. Calder: 6 January, 1939, Hahn and Strassmann reported experimental results in German publication. No explanation of failure to separate radioactive products of uranium-neutron reaction by barium precipitation.

E. Orr: That same month, I came to U. S., talked to Einstein at Princeton. Selina cabled verifying process she named "fission." U-235 atom splits, get two barium atoms plus one hundred megavolts.

E. Ferrini: Best thing is, another neutron comes from the fission.

E. Orr: And that neutron hits another U-235 atom, perhaps.

E. Ferrini: Which also fissions, maybe.

A. Calder: Depends on using only U-235, no other isotopes of uranium. If any U-238 present, eats up intermediate energy neutrons. Natural purified uranium can't be used for chain reaction. Must separate U-235; very difficult.

H. MacLaurin: So Nazis probably don't have bomb now.

K. Zimas: Correct, because of difficulty of separating isotopes of uranium, which have same chemical properties. New development, however: 11 July last year, Ornberg at Radiation Lab found neutrons of intermediate speed bombarding U-238 nucleii make PU-239, plutonium. Tests by Ornberg: plutonium has same fissionable properties as U-235, different chemical properties. Therefore separates easily. Reported to Nat. Acad. of Sciences.

N. Nachtigall: To the point. Bang. Boom. Harold wants to hear how he fits in.

A. Calder: Plutonium bomb? Possible, yes. The plutonium made from chain-reacting pile using moderator of graphite or heavy water. Slows fast neutrons to intermediate range. Nazis have captured Norsk heavy water plant, reported stepped up output.

E. Ferrini: Race with Nazi labs. Reported Heisenberg is leader of German project.

N. Nachtigall: These aren't Harold's problems.

A. Calder: Besides chemical and physical problems separating fissionable materials, our problems: how to detonate a chain reaction? Probably will go off spontaneously when given size sphere of given purity material assembled. Analogous to the problem in storing fodder in a silo: surface area to volume determines what fraction of heat flux produced within escapes surface. In this case, neutron flux.

N. Nachtigall: Harold couldn't care less. Everything up to now our problems, atomic physicists' problems. He's a gas dynamicist. To the point, to the point.

A. Calder: Atomic bomb likely to be made by suddenly assembling critical size of fissionable material using conventional TNT explosives. After reaction starts, problem will be keeping unexploded fissionable material within mutual range for effective chain reaction. Must not merely pop and scatter reactants before they go off. This is gas dynamics problem of unprecedented importance in war effort.

N. Nachtigall: What he's trying to say: are you willing to devote your energies through duration of project to these questions? Means living in isolated places in South, Southwest. May be long periods without family. Probably inconvenience, discomfort. Even so, likely to be greatest scientific challenge of your life.

H. MacLaurin: Yes.

N. Nachtigall: Thanks, H. Promise you exciting times.

chapter three

IN THE EARLY MONTHS OF 1943, as a particularly uncomfortable winter was ending, a variety of uneasy feelings came to my mother, and she often called my father home from his office in the middle of the day. They went together and looked at the slum house in Cambridge near Central Square where my father had roomed as a graduate student and my mother had lived with her roommates downstairs. They stood beside the locomotives at South Station arriving from the Midwest, and my mother would point out, as the red dusk illuminated steam and smoke above the train — the orange and blue colors making it appear to be a carnival train — the car she must have stepped out of on her first arrival in Boston fifteen years earlier. In the Fens behind Back Bay they walked miles on the concrete paths over which they had pushed my carriage, and since my mother was only infrequently disposed to prepare dinner, they ate often at an austere Swedish self-service restaurant. There no one spoke or smiled, and the high, smooth ceiling and yellow walls gave back only the

17

sounds of the solitary eaters' dishes and tableware. On one occasion they visited the bar on Washington Street where they had so often met their friends during my father's graduate student days, and although they hardly expected to meet any of the old college friends my mother's uncomfortable nostalgia had pushed them to seek there, they were not prepared to spend their evening listening to the bartender berate his glass-washing assistant. "You're a winner, Charlie," he called again and again, winking at my parents as if he expected them to join in. "You're one of a kind." And Charlie broke the glasses as if this were what he was being paid for.

My father began his involvement with the new project in a series of week-long trips to Tennessee. Until he received a kind of official warning, his shoes were invariably caked with thick red mud when he returned to Boston. This mud was becoming the emblem of the secret project researcher until someone important told them all to clean their shoes before they took the train north.

As the spring began, my mother's disposition improved. She began getting the meals regularly, even through the long weeks when my father was absent. The little dust pets that made their homes under the furniture suffered more regular pogroms, and we listened often to classical music on the phonograph. In April, as my mother was becoming big, my father left us for a period of work in Tennessee which he reluctantly told us would be long.

Something reversed then for my mother, and the desolate expressions she had worn in the winter months returned. A storm brought a gutter down outside of one of our windows, causing it to hang at a crazy angle and move in the wind. My mother refused to look out of the window until the gutter was repaired, and as she waited for the landlord to make good his promise to send the repairmen, she wept. A six-page letter came from her mother telling how her father had been humiliatingly fired from his factory job. Sent home sick by the company medical office, her father had stopped at the bar where his brother worked to borrow a dollar for cab fare. At that moment, two company supervisors who had been following his taxi burst in and fired him on the spot, using abusive language and threatening him with their fists. No one knew what he would do now, as he had been an employee of that same firm for fifteen years and owed money to their credit union.

In late May, at the end of the school term, my mother decided we would go to Tennessee and spend a month with my father before the baby was due. The route the train took carrying us south was a route one had little trouble imagining Lincoln's funeral train rolling over: shy green hills standing beside the tracks; fences, cattle; the illusion of people watching us, watching the train move slowly through the stations without stopping. It was hot. The big green broadness of the American southern states was letting us come in. Passing over rivers on wooden trestles, the train ran above thick green treetops, leaving below either red rivers or green oceans. My mother lost her purse in the dining car, and although a Negro porter and a conductor pressed themselves into the service of searching for it all over the train, it could not be found. The porter cheerfully loaned my mother thirty dollars, which she was embarrassed but constrained to accept. He left his name and address with her with a smile so genuine and hospitable that he appeared to expect nothing more from her later than a postcard.

Oak Ridge came as a blow to my mother. It was dirty and

uncomfortable, and she saw little of my father, since he was out of town all day at the site. The construction site was, of course, off limits to her, and she found little to do in Oak Ridge during the day. Her conviction to endure the insects, flooded streets, and boredom of Oak Ridge lasted exactly one week, at the end of which she moved to a hotel in Knoxville. I stayed with my father at the hotel in Oak Ridge during the week, and we visited my mother in her civilization on weekends, Saturday noon to Sunday night. These brief periods were inevitably turbulent, and the entire project of my mother's trip to Tennessee began to look ill-conceived. My father and I were always eager to leave the mawkish elegance of her Knoxville hotel on Sunday evenings and return to the tents and trailers of our friends in Oak Ridge, where people drank beer and played music in enormous woodwind and brass ensembles as the rain came down in the dark night outside.

It happened that my father and I were guests in someone's trailer the night my mother gave birth, and we never knew my little sister had been born until the following day when a telephone message reached us. My father's friend Nelson Nachtigall came to our aid and found us some emergency transportation to Knoxville that afternoon: it was with a soldier who was ferrying a dilapidated pickup truck there for maintenance. Before we could leave the motor pool, the soldier's wife called to tell him that she had won a prize on a radio quiz program in Knoxville and asked him to pick it up. We drove first to the studios of the radio station, which were located over a hash house. There the soldier confronted an individual who introduced himself as Cousin Frankie, and they looked together all over the studio for the prize, Cousin Frankie stopping every so often to begin another record and spray his dialect-ridden patter out over the airwaves. They found the prize, a canned ham, under a pile of cardboard boxes. Cousin Frankie introduced the soldier on the air as a devoted fan of the radio station and the soldier gave a fifteen-minute testimonial for the station. The soldier said that he and his wife were moving out of the state soon because they were being transferred, and Cousin Frankie felt sorry for himself for losing his audience. When we left, the soldier told us he had never listened to that station before in his life.

My little sister, born nearly a month prematurely, was given a slim chance to live. She was extremely small and frail, and the doctor my father spoke to said there were eating problems and breathing problems, but still there was hope. My father and I took up residence in my mother's hotel room, where she came to convalesce after about a week. The baby had to stay in the hospital much longer. My mother needed and appreciated the attention my father stayed in Knoxville to give her, but eventually the pressures of his work pushed him back to Oak Ridge for all but the weekends, as before. My mother chafed under what she took to be his neglect of her, and there were unreasonable, unbearable fights.

On a Sunday in late June, my parents found themselves sitting on the bench of a roofed-in picnic table in a park outside Knoxville, discussing their separation. The first drops of one of those arbitrary summer storms were beginning to fall, and nearby a small girl was taking leave of her three friends.

"Call me up tonight," they said to her as she walked away without a word. "Call me up tonight, O.K. Janie?" But they didn't mean it and Janie didn't answer.

When I was asked with whom I wanted to live, I chose my

father and insisted on this choice despite his encouragement to return to Boston. Soon afterwards, when my little sister was judged strong enough to travel, my mother took her away on the train.

But by then, my father had already met Maryann.

chapter four

TERRIBLE NEWS, MARYANN. I've suffered a very painful sunburn painting my parents' barn. This is only one reason the
painting and scraping job is going badly. The scraping, my
father says, is necessary everywhere, and I have done an experiment on one patch of siding under the eaves which proves
this is true. Even when the scraping has been done, two coats
of paint seem to do nothing on the old, porous wood. I dangle
from the ladder through a morning, and only my shadow
seems to be making progress across the wall. Once I thought I
could just begin this job somewhere and see it through to the
end, but now I'm not so sure.

Has it been fifteen years since we were together? Yes. I
haven't seen you since 1945. I've been through college since
then. I've completed a legitimate scientific education in prep-
aration for a career in research. You may have heard this
from someone, although I can't think who might have told
you. What you wonder is what am I doing here at my parents'
house working every day on their barn? This should be only

temporary, although I've been at it for the past seven months. I had a technical job, but it wasn't working out. You'll want to know about that, but could I leave it for the moment? Just now I'd like to join you back in Oak Ridge, late in the summer of 1943, when I was thirteen and you and my father were barely acquainted.

Of course, you and he had been enjoying each other's company for several weeks before that evening you invited us for dinner in your trailer. Do you recall the day? I can't keep them straight: it was some time about a month after my mother's departure. My father and I had been living in town at the old wooden hotel, somewhere in the center of town. Big columns on the porch, heavy branches outside the windows. Maybe you can help me with the name: I've forgotten it if I ever knew it. During the days, when he was working out at the site, I was taken to the house of a lady in the town to be minded until he came for me in the evenings. This lady, whose name, you remember, was Mrs. Brummel, had seen you and my father together so often that I suppose she naturally assumed you were my mother. In a way, this may have been your fault, for you never did anything to correct Mrs. Brummel's impression of our relationship.

On this evening when we were to visit you in your trailer, you and my father drove up in your old Buick in front of Mrs. Brummel's house, and as always I came out to meet you. Mrs. Brummel followed me out the door, but only in time to see me climbing into your car.

"Hello, Mrs. Brummel!" you called from the driver's seat. The side of your Buick was covered with mud in a mountainous pattern which started near the front mudguard and climbed evenly over the crest of the rear fenders.

"Hello, Mrs. and Mr. MacLaurrer," Mrs. Brummel said.

24

She drew closer to your car, pushing her way through a swinging gate in the fence which surrounded her house.

"I can never say your name," she said through a grin which was out of proportion with the levity of the occasion. "How do you say your name, MacLaurrer? You wrote it for me once; is the last letter an 'r' or an 'n'? You should have my name, simple: Brummel. Then everyone can say it." By this time she was leaning in the window at you, Maryann, and although I think you tried to give her some reply to her question, she didn't give you any time to speak.

"Oh, and you have your husband with you," she went on. "You've just come from wherever it is that you're working out there? I wish you'd tell me what you're up to! That man who works in Goodsell's store told me today that you were making the front ends of horses for the cavalry, and they were going to be shipped to Chicago to be put together. That's what he said, but I don't know what to believe!"

My father was sitting in the middle of the front seat, leaning forward a little in order to see Mrs. Brummel.

"I know you can't tell me what you do out there," Mrs. Brummel was saying. Then, seeing me, her charge of the whole day, sitting beside my father on the far side of the front seat, she had an inspiration: "But you can tell Timmy, and Timmy can whisper it to me when he comes to see me tomorrow!"

Ironically, I did have a secret to whisper to Mrs. Brummel, but the matters which I had contemplated taking up with her had to do with her own personal hygiene, not the construction out at the site.

"Oh, you'll be wanting to go on, now, and I'm keeping you. You'll be wanting to have your supper, and Timmy will want his. How happy you three look together! You remind me of my husband and myself when we were young. Go on, go on; I'm not too old to remember!"

So at last we did go on. You drove us off, Maryann. You snapped on the radio and swung us quickly through the trees.

"I hate the time it takes to warm up," you said, speaking of the radio. "It takes so long to warm up." But very shortly Jo Stafford was upon us, singing "You Are" to the accompaniment of the big Miller orchestra. "You are . . ." Jo Stafford sang, and it was true: we were. Hickory trees, and pine trees, and elms were . . . they were all around us. The Clinch River, Happy Valley coming toward us . . . all these things were, too. But most of all, Maryann, you, with your lovely smile irreverently mimicking the Buick's speedometer face, you, who had turned on Jo Stafford but now were listening only to the low sound of my father talking, *you* were. Are.

We found Happy Valley just as the sun was going down, and with it, we found five thousand house trailers. At last the red mud which had been splashed on the side of your car matched the color of the mud on the ground. Your trailer was at the end of a long line in the so-called low amenity area. The Buick stopped, its mudguards dripping, on a plot adjacent to your trailer, and we got out. A humble little concrete slab made a place for us to wipe our feet before we went inside. Even so, we all removed our shoes and left them outside. You excused yourself and went into what I supposed to be the bathroom, Maryann. When you came out, you were wearing a simple housedress and your hair was done in two braids, fastened at the ends with rubber bands.

"Hiya, Pigtails!" my father said.

"Big what?" you snapped.

"Tails," my father repeated, putting his hand on your

shoulder, for now you were both in your tiny kitchen making the supper. "Pigtails," he said again.

"Oh, I thought you said *big* something." And I heard both of you laughing. For all Mrs. Brummel's lack of information in other matters, I did have to admit that she was right, that you did look happy.

Do you remember what you served us for dinner that evening? I'll bet you'll be surprised how well *I* remember. You served a baked chicken dish with sweet potatoes, and we had a bottle of red wine, some of which my father spilled on the floor when he opened it.

"Never mind," you said. "Never mind. Any spot we get on the floor will just blend in with all the other spots. All the mud around here is sort of red, anyway."

"Here, I can get it up," my father insisted, pulling out his handkerchief.

"No, absolutely not," you said. "If the Army was foresighted enough to paint all these trailers the color of dirt, it's not up to us to defeat their purpose by wiping up spots."

"You think olive drab is the color of dirt?"

"Somebody's dirt, I suppose. Not our dirt. I don't know," you said thoughtfully. "I don't think any color is exactly the color of dirt."

"I don't want to talk about dirt," my father said. "I want to talk about you. I want to find out about you."

"What would you like to *find out* about me?"

"Anything. I don't really know a thing about you. We never talk about ourselves. Whether you have any brothers and sisters, or if you have a dog at home."

"I don't have a dog at home," you began. "I do have an older brother. He went to Brown and got married, and now he

27

lives up in your part of the country, in New York. I used to have a younger sister. She drowned."

"I'm sorry."

"There's no need for *you* to be sorry. I like to remember my sister. Don't be sorry that you asked me about her; I like to be asked about her."

"I was asking about you."

"There's practically nothing about me. I've studied dancing. I like that. My mother and father wanted me to go to secretarial school, so I went last year. I didn't go back this year, though."

"Why?"

"I didn't like any of it. It seemed as if I were just wasting my parents' money, and they haven't got it to waste. The girls that got ahead there were the ones you wouldn't want to know. My friends were all flunking out; most of them left sooner than I did. If I went back there this year, I wouldn't know a single person."

"Did you want to be a secretary?"

"Not so as you'd notice."

There was a candle on the table, and I was watching its flame. The trailer was in darkness except for this candle and a small night-lamp over the bunks.

"Timmy looks like he's going to fall fast asleep," you told my father. Both of you moved practically without sound in the darkness, making the upper bunk ready for me. When you finished, my father helped me into it and took my shoes, one by one, as I handed them to him. My father implied, by his tone of voice, that it would be unreasonable for me to ask him for a pair of pajamas, so I did not. From my bunk I could see the shadow of your braids on the wooden wall, but I couldn't see the candlelight on your face, Maryann.

"Now you'll want to know about me," my father said, when you were both seated at the table again.

"No, I already know about you. Now I want to know about Timmy's mother."

"Oh, dirt again," my father said, unwisely.

"No. *Not* dirt. See if you can be fair to me. Think of me like a scientific problem. You have to tell me something about Timmy's mother and where I stand. Tell me as much as you think I have to know."

Your braids made two more wicks for the candle's light. My father took a cigarette from his package and rolled it between his fingers, as if looking for the seam. The cigarette had a dark side, like the moon.

"In a few weeks, Timmy and I are going to have to move to New Mexico. For the time being, Timmy's mother is unable," my father said, cycling the unlit cigarette over and over between his fingers, ". . . unable to decide to come with us. She may never come with us."

"No?"

Your hair parted, Maryann, in a lovely line which nonchalantly pointed to the collar of your housedress. The rubberbanded ends of your braids lay on your shoulders.

"How long are you going to stay?"

"As long as it takes. Perhaps a year."

"I haven't anything to do for a year," you said. "I guess I'll come with you."

"Well," my father said, "give it some thought. We'll live in a new town where there will certainly be a number of hardships. Still, it would be wonderful to have you."

And that's all I remember about your lovely dinner in the trailer: our New Mexico days at their beginning. This thought of beginnings seems especially relevant to me now, because in the last year or so there has been someone with whom I could make a beginning, a lovely girl I could marry. Shall I tell you about her? What do you want to know? She is tall and wears her hair long. She paints. She rides a bicycle through heavy Boston traffic. She likes pot. She's apparently willing to risk her life with me. She reminds me of you.

I often think, Maryann, that some day you're going to come back to me and suggest that we start our trip to New Mexico all over again. You'll forget that I've grown up and that my father and mother are reconciled, and you'll ask my father and me to ask you again, and so we shall: "Will you come with us?" But even if this should happen; even if we three should take advantage of a coincidence of holidays some time in the future to meet and begin our journey across the country again; if we should do it all a second time, how would that be better than having only done it once?

chapter five

TWICE A WEEK, I get out of the barn the old Rambler station wagon my father lets me drive and make the trip to Boston, where at the Massachusetts General Hospital Social Service Facility I spend an hour talking with Mr. Grey, who has a degree in I think psychiatric social work. He is not a difficult sort of person, but I've established that he thinks a great deal of himself for not having joined a fraternity in college. I'm beginning to understand that there is a whole group of people who do competent work in positions of modest prestige like Mr. Grey, and who are in all other ways generous and charitable, yet imagine that their chief moral credit derives from the fact that they didn't join a fraternity in college. Mr. Grey tries to talk to me about science, but it doesn't go very far. If I happen to be carrying a textbook which I have borrowed from the library, he compliments me on how difficult the title sounds. The fact that I am still planning a career in research encourages him.

The drive to Boston from the community of Dover, where

we live, takes me first along country roads lined with stone walls of an old, neat, puritan construction, and then along a faster road through the centers of Newton and Wellesley. When I can be bothered to think about the larger stones in the walls, their size and grace, what I like to imagine about them is their riding along on the glaciers, getting on in the darkness of the northern latitudes, the scooped-out floor of Hudson Bay for example, and getting off in New England, where the glacier is beginning to look like a dirty, low, late April snowbank.

Mr. Grey often wants to start our discussions with the job I had after college and why it didn't work out. This isn't my favorite subject. On hot summer mornings as I drive to keep my appointment with him, the road makes slick mirages ahead of the car and I find myself supposing that he will begin with this subject again. The job was with a company on Route 128 which made electronic hardware for the military, microwave components mostly. It thought it had something for junior physicists to do, but it really didn't. There you could park your car in the white-hot parking lot on a day like this and enter the building (showing your badge to the geriatrics case at the door) and pass offices where the electric fans were already on and the engineers, uniformly wearing white shirts and slim ties, their jackets removed, leaned on filing cabinets and exchanged real estate information and building materials prices. They all liked electric fans. They liked to have them on. They considered an electric fan something worth fighting over. Through the afternoons they would look in the newspaper to see what jobs were going for more money elsewhere.

The uniform of the physicist, as opposed to the engineer, went a little more in the direction of V-necked sweaters over the white shirt and tie (broader tie), but a sweater was impossible to keep on in the summer, so between May and September you could take your tie off when you got to the office and walk around with your shirt collar open. Physicists who went around in miracle fabric shirts with their collars open and their European undershirts visible beneath the sheer cloth also tended to have graduate degrees, and their eating lunch together, that is, without me, advised me against copying their dress really all the way. Another thing that distressed me was that I found myself plotting a lot of graphs for them. Asking a man to plot a graph for you, even if it's an emergency and you ask him with an embarrassed chuckle in your voice, isn't a way of showing your regard for him.

By the time I had worked for the company a year, I discovered I had plotted seventy-seven graphs for fourteen different people, not counting the ones I had plotted for myself in connection with the research project on traveling wave tubes I was supposed to be carrying out. (Mr. Grey asks me here if this was when I started spending so much time on the toilet. I tell him no, this was the beginning of my period of taking work outside in the high grass.)

The physicists who were supposed to be supervising me didn't really approve of my taking work outside. I made a point, however, of showing them that the work I did out there was their graphs, and the fact that I was accomplishing these graphs and not sleeping made the arrangement look practical. The badge-checking guard would watch me from his dark doorway with alcohol-jaundiced eyes. I worked under a tree on a little rise to the west of the parking lot, balancing a small drafting board on my knees. Insects making their way through the high grass sometimes jumped on my graph paper. This had to come to an end in the fall with the arrival of cooler weather and a certain undisguised impatience with me on the part of my supervisors. I moved back into the office I shared with three other people, each man to a wall, in one of the windowless spaces illuminated by fluorescent fixtures on the ground floor. My only friend there was a sad sack by the name of Dick who told me many stories about his Navy experiences, most of which had sadistic overtones. He was twenty-three years old, married, and had three children. His wife called him so often in the day that everyone referred to his extension as the "hot line." My graph-drawing assignments were now augmented by sessions on the desk calculator. One of my physicist-patrons discovered a consistent calculational error in a series of graphs I had required a month to construct, and lost his humor in discussing it with me.

And so it happened that I came to need a place to rest at intermediate moments in the day. With the alternative of taking my work outside now removed, and considering the economy with which the plant designers had budgeted floor space, I had very few choices of places to hide. Perhaps more important was my own feeling about hiding: I didn't want to steal time from my job so much as I wanted to find a kind of refreshing surroundings which could allow me to consider certain matters to the benefit of both myself and my job. The nature of this place would have to relieve me of any feeling of guilt for not carrying a slide rule there: it should be a place where manipulative, as opposed to cognitive, work would be impossible.

This is how I came to dawdle at stool. It began during a period of real physical constipation, when entirely official business would bring me to the toilet for the better part of a morning or afternoon. In the beginning, the only reading material I would have for these hours were the electronics trade journals with their three-color advertisements for expensive measuring instrumentation and their remarkably right-thinking "Views from Washington" which had been left there by the engineers. Some of the advertisements featured photographs of electronic black boxes hand-held by lightly clad Texas blondes with white teeth. But the stack of magazines was renewed only very infrequently, and I soon found it to my advantage to have a book in the breast pocket of my coat when I made my visit.

The books I read there were the books I had read in childhood, and the feelings of transportation, of removal, of installation in the world of the fiction on the page were sometimes identical with the feelings I had experienced before, so soon after I had learned to read. This success wasn't entirely to my own credit. I had going for me a number of circumstances which assisted me in regaining the pleasure of the child reader: the social isolation, the confined posture, the appetite for escape, the mild threat of interruption. Upon finishing many of the books familiar from an earlier reading, I started the Tom Swift series, which I knew my father had read when he was young, and wondered how I had overlooked them until now.

My friend Dick would come and call me to the telephone or bring me a message that so-and-so was looking for me when the need arose. He would also come sometimes and speak to me through the door even when there wasn't a message. He would report what he had heard said about me among the physicists who were supposed to be supervising me, but who could no longer supervise me because I had arranged to supervise myself. From his comments I could understand that they were concerned about me and were making a dedicated effort to improve my job so that I could be happier at it. There was a period when I was assigned to what most people considered the prize project at the laboratory, electron gun design in the electrolytic tank. I did enjoy this somewhat more, but by then my pattern of being unavailable for a large fraction of the day was firmly established. Dick brought me more distressing rumors, and my bowels grew harder than before.

Early in the March of my second year at the plant, I was given what amounted to a hearing by three of the physicists who had been receiving my services. They were very polite and deferential to me, but they told me they believed I was having a nervous breakdown and in my own best interests they were sacking me.

chapter six

T HE M ASSACHUSETTS G ENERAL H OSPITAL has slighted Mr. Grey in the accommodations it provides him, but he doesn't seem to mind. The secretary he shares with several other people is quite unattractive and dull. His office has no window except the frosted glass in his door, and his own desk and chair so nearly fill the floor space that I imagine he has to hand his waste paper out the door to his secretary when something comes along which has to be thrown away.

Mr. Grey is naturally interested in what I have told him about Maryann. I wanted him to develop a firm impression about her before he undertook helping me, and this seems to have been accomplished. From the skill he is building in asking questions about her, I think he is beginning to know her. He has asked me where she is now. I tell him that for the moment she is lost. I don't know her address. If I did, I would write to her.

"Let me suggest a game to you," Mr. Grey said recently. "In this game, you and I will find Maryann just the same way we would find anything else you had lost. We'll go back to the point you remember having Maryann, and then we'll try to remember where you put her. I want you to *be* Maryann at Oak Ridge, working alone in her cubicle. What is she thinking?"

"She's thinking that she's Prince Albert in a can," I said.

Mr. Grey looked bored by what I had said. "What?" he asked.

"Prince Albert in a can is something my father used to do. He told Maryann and me about it. He and his school friends would call a tobacco shop and ask if they had Prince Albert in a can. If they did, my father would say, 'You'd better let him out, he's getting awfully stuffy in there.' Then they'd hang up."

"This was when your father was very young?"

"Of course."

"And so Maryann is Prince Albert in a can because the room she works in is so small, and it's hot. What does she think about her job, and the place she has to work?"

"She doesn't like it."

"Why is that?"

"There's nothing for her to be interested in. She has to turn knobs to keep some meters within limits, and she has to call someone on a telephone when something happens. I was never really able to understand what this job was from her descriptions. She was monitoring something."

Mr. Grey was slouching in his chair in a very exaggerated position: a knee was hooked around one of the chair arms, and both of his feet were off the floor. He was trying to put me at ease with this marvelously informal posture.

"Maryann is doing this boring job in a bare little room, and let's suppose she has an opportunity to think about things

38

other than the job. What does she think about Harold Mac-
Laurin and his son?"

"She wonders what it would be like to go with them to New
Mexico."

"Is that all? Aren't there stronger feelings?"

"Yes."

"What are they? Love?"

*Love? Maryann touches her hair with a finger. The room is
hot and noisy. The steel walls are close enough for her to see
details of roughness in the paint. First the boys sat on stone
walls alone, but then the girls joined them. They played
games of capturing, pushing. They touched each other, pretending to be angry. Shouts. Touches. Combat. Later the boys
had cars, and the girls wore kerchiefs. In groups, at night,
they drove the mountain roads. Cooler in valleys, sometimes
fog, warmer on high places. And then, by the entrances to
abandoned mines, whose holes rushed deep down, there was
love. It didn't matter if the weather was cold, because then
you put your hands inside each other's clothes. You ached for
the tide of the future to come up. The pine trees had wind
noises in them, and these were simple kisses. Like the silver
foil wrapping a chocolate. Removed very carefully, in order
not to spoil . . .*

"I don't think 'love,' " I told him. "Because when you're
young, this has so much sex attached to it, and I really picture
my father and Maryann having a celibate relationship, at least
during this early time."

"Very well," Mr. Grey said, "not love. But what, then, if
she decided to come with you to New Mexico?"

"I wonder this myself," I said. "It may have simply been
that she wanted to leave town, and we were going, so she came
with us."

Mr. Grey stretched his hands up and clasped them behind his neck. "Do you want to believe that Maryann was only catching a ride with you?"

"I don't want to believe it," I said. "But it's a possibility."

Maryann, at work in her steel room, falls farther into her daydream. Night birds call from the heights of dark trees. Clay and leaves feel cold on her skin but the air is warm. Moon and stars make the sky light, and the ground has shadows moving on it. One of the other couples stirs and then is silent again.

"Would she do this?" Mr. Grey asked. "I mean, here she is at work, thinking about going to the Southwest with this older, married scientist and his young son. What's her impression of what this will be like?"

"She plans to be good to us. She's going to take care of us, because this is what she imagines we want from her."

"She's going to be loyal to you?"

"I don't think this is on her mind, really."

"She doesn't plan to be with you forever?"

"She simply doesn't think of it," I said. Mr. Grey returned his folded hands to his lap. He faced me directly, for the first time in our interview.

"And now there's no way she can be reached?"

"There's no way *I* can reach her," I said.

chapter seven

SOMEWHERE IN THE FOUNDATIONS of my parents' reconciliation is an unspoken agreement that they will both forget Maryann. I can see how this works for my mother: she never knew Maryann as anyone but a threat. Maryann hides easily for her. But how am I to understand why my father acts coy when I mention Maryann's name? Others have had the same experience: my father's friends find him vague when they speak about her. Has he really forgotten her, or was he blind to her when she was with us? We were arguing just a moment ago, after dinner, about certain specific incidents. He promised me he'd think about these, and if he does, I'm certain he'll remember Maryann.

The first incident occurred on the day of our departure from Oak Ridge. It was just before we loaded the small four-wheel-drive truck we had been assigned to drive to New Mexico. My father, who loves machinery, was so pleased with the performance of the vehicle that he invited me to come on a little adventure in it. It was morning, and the rain clouds which sometimes hang only a few hundred feet off the ground all through the summer in Tennessee were leaking water into the red mud on the ground. I say the clouds were there, and you should believe me, but if someone were absolutely dedicated to seeing a blue hole or two, and ringing this hole a few white tops of clouds, and above these the sun, then he would not have been disappointed.

My father and I sat together on the straight front seat, his hand on the gearshift, his feet nearly always on the accelerator and clutch pedals, so often did he shift. We cracked open puddles on the road with our military tires. Our windshield wipers sometimes worked so hard that they flung water from the windshield out into the road. We were sliding, sliding in the mud, sometimes sliding nearly a full circle before my father, shifting down and steering violently into the skid, would bring the truck back onto the road. I was delighted with what he was doing; I was shouting and laughing over the roar of the engine. Then he slid us a little bit too far, and suddenly we were off the road, skidding down an embankment. We came to a stop with the front end pointing up a short grade. *"I remember this part," my father said when I got this far in the story. "If you remember this part," I asked him, "why can't you remember what comes later, the Maryann part?"*

When he was satisfied that our four-wheel-drive wasn't going to get us back on the road, my father shut down the engine and we got out of the truck. He looked the situation over and spotted a tree stump near the road. "Looks like we'll have to use the old winch on this one, Timmy," he said. But even with the old winch working, and our cable wrapped around the stump ahead, the truck wouldn't move. Its wheels had dug four holes for themselves, and the vehicle was resting on its belly in the mud. We left it where it was and walked back through the puddles to Happy Valley.

"You were *playing* with it?" Maryann said when she had driven us back to the spot where the truck was mired. "You were *playing* with it when it ran off the road?" My father took several large flat boards out of the trunk of her Buick. He used one jack which was already in the truck plus Maryann's jack to lift each wheel and fill the hole in with gravel and boards. "Now she'll pull herself out," he said, and Maryann and I stood by while he tried the winch again. Maryann held the collar of her cloth coat up around her ears, lifting it so that her knees showed. The cold rain was beating harder on red earth all around us, rattling the leaves of distant trees. With the engine roaring, my father drove the truck up onto the road. Maryann and I followed him. Her teeth were chattering while he unhooked the cable from the stump. "What now?" she said when he was finished.

"Now," he said, bringing the back of his wrist out from under the sleeve of his coat, looking at his watch, "it's noon. Timmy and I have to get this thing loaded. We'll be by your place about three."

"Do you still want to leave today?"

"Why not? We can get a couple of hundred miles down the road yet today."

"O.K.," she said. "See you." And with that, the person who my father has just now begun claiming he doesn't wish to remember, the reddish-brown-haired, brown-eyed, slimmer-than-when-we-first-met-her person whose name was Maryann, got into her Buick and drove away. *"I remember now, that was Maryann, all right,"* my father admitted. *"We used her jack."*

Exactly, I told him. And later that afternoon we hitched her trailer to our truck. Down it came from its concrete posts. Its tires had to be inflated from an air bottle, and its brake light wires had to be connected. But by the end of the afternoon, there it was, ready to go. Maryann sang "Brown as a Berry from Riding the Prairie" while we were putting her kitchen supplies in cardboard boxes. Verse after verse she sang while packing away her boxes of confectioner's sugar and potholders. By the time she got to the last few choruses, my father and I had heard the refrain often enough to help her with it. We tied down everything movable in the trailer and took the mirrors off the walls. Maryann drove her car out to the house of her parents, where she was going to leave it during her New Mexico stay. It was here that we picked her up, many hours behind schedule, with the sun ready to go down. Maryann had told her parents that her job had been transferred to New Mexico, and this actually was not a lie, for my father had arranged another job for her there.

She was waiting for us on the lawn of her parents' house when we arrived. The house was small and white. Climbing flowers climbed on it, and the Cumberland Mountains grew up behind. Maryann wanted to take us somewhere before we went inside to meet her parents. She led us through her mother's flowers down a path which crossed a neighbor's yard and up a hill. At the crest of the hill, Maryann's hair lifted from her shoulders occasionally in the evening breeze. Here the path led down into the yard of an old church. We climbed another rise into a small graveyard. Maryann stopped before a small, not particularly distinguished stone cross. She knelt here and prayed for a moment, then spread her dress with her hand and sat in the long grass. We joined her.

"This is your sister's grave," my father said after a while.

"Yes," she said.

The night insects began their songs.

"I wish you'd tell me about your sister," my father said. "You've often let me believe that you were close, and now I think perhaps I won't know you until I know her. Don't tell me how she died; tell me how she lived."

"She lived," Maryann began, "happily, I suppose. Everyone said she lived in my shadow, when she was alive. That's funny. Because now it's the other way around. I sometimes imagine that we've changed places, that she's living my life. If I'm doing something, something she liked to do, like wading or dancing, I get so that I believe she's doing it instead of me. She's the one who's really doing it. I'm happiest when I feel that."

We were silent for a short time. My father picked grass stalks and chewed them. "Aren't things fun when you're yourself, too?"

"Not particularly," Maryann said.

"Why?" my father asked her. "Don't you have any legitimacy yourself? Everyone does. You do."

"Nope," Maryann said. She hugged her knees with her skirt.

"Baloney," my father said.

Maryann said she suspected that she was an illegitimate child, that her parents had married only after her birth. Her dead sister, she said, had been the only legitimate child of the marriage. Her parents had never told her the truth of this, but her school friends, if they knew nothing else, always seemed to know this story. Maryann had developed a deep jealousy of her sister, a jealousy which was always restless and sometimes murderous. Many of her favorite dreams somehow involved usurping her sister's place. But when her sister died in the accident, when she drowned, this wasn't part of the plan. Her sister came instead to take her place in life, in the best parts of life, in happiness.

When we returned to the Moriartys' house, the rain, which had begun again, spattered off the eaves into the lush flowerbed. We visited with Maryann's parents for half an hour, drinking tea from a porcelain tea set. I could see out the window into the dark foothills of the oldest mountains in our country. Mr. Moriarty, a miner, had face and hands with mining dirt worked into the skin so deep that no soap would wash it away. I looked around their living room to see if he had brought his shovel home with him, but it was not in evidence.

"I'm glad to see you get ahead," Mrs. Moriarty told her daughter as we were preparing to leave. "It's hard for a woman to get ahead today unless she has a gorgeous body. With so many men, the first thing they look at when a woman enters a room is to see how she's built."

We were outside again, driving through the dark rain, when my father spoke. "What did your mother have in mind with that remark?"

"Who knows? Perhaps she thinks I'm setting off for a place where I'll be exploited."

"Is that where you think you're going?"

"Hardly. Things turn out for me. People take care of me. I think I must evoke the daughter image or something."

The rain battered on the roof and our military tires hummed across Tennessee. Maryann read directions to my father from a road map she had unfolded in her lap. We stopped at a small store and filled our gas tank. My father bought candy bars for us all and we pushed on.

46

"Your parents' house reminds me of our apartment in Boston," my father said.

"Oh? What were you thinking about it?"

"I was thinking I'm not there now."

"And that's all?"

"No, I suppose I was reminded about the worries of that place. I used to worry about it all the time: Supposing the chimney collapses, what if I've forgotten to pay the rent, maybe my marriage is going down the drain."

"You worry about things like that?"

"I worry about them more when I'm near them. But even now I have these suspicions."

Maryann was playing with a rubber band wound around her fingers. Her silence gave us the impression that she thought it was foolish to worry about things you couldn't help.

"But now all this new work has come up for me, Maryann. I've been invited to think about the biggest scientific . . ." he searched for words, ". . . *chance*, the biggest *chance* I've ever taken."

Maryann and I answered him with more silence. He decided to dab at his masterpiece again, as if he had just thought of the exact stroke which would finish it.

"The more I think about this new problem that we're all involved in, the more I see of these fantastic people I'm working with, the farther I go from the old troubles, the old worries; the farther I go from what I had before."

"Houses, wives."

"More than that."

We took him at his word and rolled on through the darkness.

chapter eight

OUR FIRST MORNING ON THE ROAD was so bright and wet that if I described it in any detail, you would be sure to think I was lying, or at least compromising the truth. When my father opened the door of the trailer, morning sunshine slapped all of us in the face. From my high bunk, I saw the light strike the floor of the trailer. Pools of water outside our door shone like mirrors.

Maryann discovered that our trailer grounds were adjacent to a grass airport. As my father set up the Coleman stove and the breakfast table outside on the grass, Maryann and I walked to a low stone wall, beyond which the activities of the airport were going on. When breakfast was ready, Maryann suggested that we bring our plates across the stone wall and sit on the edge of the airfield to eat. I helped my father work the pat of yellow coloring into a package of margarine. (It came from the store bone-white and you were expected to complete the counterfeit at home.) Airplanes flew nearly over our heads as we carried our food and the tablecloth to the point Maryann had designated.

While we were eating, a little dot appeared in the sky and started making a rasping, buzzing noise. We all looked at the dot; Maryann commented that it was awfully loud for an airplane so far away. As my father finished kneading the margarine into a homogeneous, buttery color, the airplane grew closer and turned several times in the air, treating us to a variety of ear-splitting engine and propeller noises. Maryann lifted her chin to follow its progress. The sun above us first made the sky blue, then made the airplane's wings flash at us, and then whitened Maryann's neck. My father spread the margarine on several pieces of bread, lined half of these with sardines, and then put their lids on. He passed us our sandwiches. The airplane landed, taxied toward a metal-clad building which supported a wind sock, and stopped in front of a car which held the members of at least two generations of a family. A wife, some children, and a grandmother greeted the pilot, whose name was painted on the side of the airplane: Poupolatos. Mr. Poupolatos walked around his airplane, opening up the gasoline caps. He told the line boy at some length which tanks he wanted filled. His children followed him on his circuit of the airplane.

"All your life," we heard the grandmother saying across the distance, "you've had the loudest machine, Georgie. When you were a boy, you had the loudest motorcycle. Then you had the loudest car. Now you have to have the loudest airplane."

Mr. Poupolatos put a cigarette in his mouth, crumpled up the empty pack, and threw it on the ground in front of his airplane. I am freakishly reminded, as I think of this, of Western movies I've seen where the white-hat gives some inexpensive comfort to his horse after he has arrived: a pat on the flank upon leaving the saddle, or the thoughtfulness of hitching him where he can reach a watering trough. Even after the Poupolatos family had driven off, all three of us, my father, Maryann, and myself, waited to see what the airplane was going to do with the empty cigarette pack lying before it on the ground. It stood faithfully still.

Later, on the road we almost passed two Spanish-looking girls hitchhiking. Maryann said quickly that she thought we should stop, and my father braked the truck nearly to a standstill before he realized that she meant we ought to stop for the hitchhikers. He took his foot off the brake and let us drift for a moment, deliberating. Then he said, "What the hell," and we stopped. Maryann held the door open while the girls ran to catch up to us.

"I guess you'd better not bring that cigarette in with you," my father said to one of the Spanish girls as she was climbing through the door. The girl took one more long drag and threw the butt outside on the ground. "Military regulations, you know," my father said. Maryann leaned forward as the two squeezed past her into the back.

"How far can we take you?" my father asked them.

"How far are you going?" the nonsmoking one returned. My father leaned across Maryann and helped slam the door. I could tell by the expression on his face that he felt challenged.

"We might get as far as Tulsa tonight," my father said. The girls pondered the offer between themselves in the back seat, talking in Spanish and using certain visual aids, one of these being a map and the other being a piece of paper with something written on it.

"O.K.," they said.

My father put the truck in gear and we were off again. The

Arkansas countryside shook dense groves of trees, some of them flowering, at our windshield. We crossed a series of little bridges in synchronization with a pair of railroad tracks running to our right. Maryann told us about the giant wood ticks which fell out of the trees onto the backs of dogs and horses. I asked her if they ever got on people, and she said, "Of course," and told me how you have to hold a rag soaked with kerosene against them to make them come off. She said they looked like moles when they got on people. I looked out on the thick trees with their shiny leaves and imagined wood ticks hiding there. Farms and farmers on tractors came and went.

In a short time, we stopped at a service station. My father got out and went sniffing around the truck as a lanky Arkansas boy put gas in our tank.

"Oh, brother!" my father said, on his hands and knees looking under the truck. Maryann slid across the seat into the driver's place and looked out at him.

"What is it?" she asked. My father came up into the hunkered position, a kind of super deep-knee-bend where you sit on your heels. He looked up at her with this hangdog smile on his face and said, "Come see this." We got out and looked where he was pointing.

"This hanger bearing has frozen up and torn its support right out. See how the whole thing turns in the hole?"

"It's not supposed to do that?" Maryann asked.

"No," my father said, standing up. "It's not supposed to do that." He looked up at the sun, and then at his watch, as if he had been given a navigational instead of a mechanical problem to do. Crickets in the trees all around deliberately distracted him with all kinds of conflicting advice. The girls in the back talked to each other, unaware of any particular crisis. The Arkansas boy wanted us to move the truck away from the pumps, and this we did. Before my father could finish inventing a strategy to deal with this contingency, a new complication arrived in the person of Mr. Poupolatos, whose family car had drawn up behind us at the pumps.

"What is it, a universal?" Mr. Poupolatos asked, joining my father on his knees and leaning under the truck. He overlooked introducing himself.

"Hanger bearing."

"Man!" Mr. Poupolatos whistled. "That's seized pretty tight, isn't it?" He took hold of the driveshaft and rattled it in the hole which it had left in the bearing mount. Klong! klong! it went, and for a moment, because of my father's position under the truck, I was alarmed, thinking that I might be hearing blows to my father's head. My fears were dismissed when both men backed out and stood up, Mr. Poupolatos clapping the dust off his hands onto his trousers. They faced each other as if in the midst of conversation, but my father was too busy thinking to speak. Mr. Poupolatos was framing something in his mouth which was probably meant to be a blank offer of help, but instead came out: "Where are you headed?"

"We were thinking about getting to Tulsa," my father admitted, for the second time that day revealing more of his expectations than he wanted to.

"Better stop thinking about that."

"Is there a GM truck place around here?"

"My brother-in-law has the dealership in Shelton," Mr. Poupolatos said. "I can probably get the parts for you, but I won't guarantee he'll have anyone there to put them in."

"I can put them in."

"You've got the tools and everything, then?" Mr. Poupolatos said with his hands on his hips, as if he were resting from the job before it was even started.

"Yes," my father told him, and disappeared back under the truck. "Let me try to get you the numbers for those parts."

It was agreed that Maryann would ride to Shelton with Mr. Poupolatos to get our parts while my father dismantled the old ones from the truck. She obtained some money from my father, took her purse from the cab, slid in beside Mr. Poupolatos in his sedan, and rode off with him.

The morning wore on with my father on his back under the truck, banging and cursing at the rusty bolts. Butterflies waved at each other from opposite ends of a grazing pasture across the road where horses were naively walking under the dangerous trees. The girls inside the truck at last acknowledged our emergency by declaring an informal end to the smoking ban my father had imposed earlier. They filled the inside of the cab with a bluish cloud. I sat on the pavement by my father and kept my eyes open for falling wood ticks which might be taking advantage of a propitious breeze to make their way toward my head.

"We used to do mechanics' work here," the Arkansas boy volunteered in a spare moment, "but there wasn't enough work to keep a man busy." My father overlooked the possible implication that the job he was presently engaged in wasn't enough to keep a man busy. "We used to have a tow truck and all, and when there'd be an accident, three of the garages around here would hear about it on the police radio and race a crew out. We used to have fights at the scene of the accident," he said, more or less to me, for I was the only one listening to him. I watched a bee buzz around his head and fly off down the highway. "Chain fights," the boy finished, grinning. He slapped his windshield-wiping rag viciously at the gasoline pumps, making them howl presumably as he had made his adversaries howl in the days of glory gone by.

When my father had removed the diseased hanger bearing and support from the driveshaft, he came out into the sunshine again, dragging his prize behind him. The Arkansas boy knelt and fingered the blackened parts, working over them as if he were a paid healer instead of just a volunteer. He rubbed bits of dirt under his fingernails joyfully, all the while maintaining the ruse of consultant. After performing every bit of first aid short of tasting the grease, he announced: "I think we have one of these out in the junkyard."

"Oh?" my father said. "Where's the junkyard?"

"This way," the Arkansas boy said, leading the way behind the station. "I think there's still a good one on an old GM truck out there, if they didn't change them on your year . . ."

In three hours, my father was finishing his installation of the perfectly good hanger bearing and support he and the Arkansas boy had found in the junkyard. I looked up and down the highway for Mr. Poupolatos' car, expecting Maryann to show up at any moment with the now-redundant truck parts. I tried to picture the expression on her face when we told her the job was finished. But Maryann didn't come, even though my father was getting ready to put the last cotter pins into his assembly. The Spanish girls got out of the truck and watched us.

"Is your girl coming back?" the bold one asked my father. He didn't answer; I suppose he didn't hear.

"Hey, gringo," she said louder, provoking a volley of tittering from her mate, "Your girl coming back?"

"Certainly she's coming back," my father said, from under the truck.

"She didn't have no wedding ring like yours. She don't have to come back if she don't want to." More tittering. My father's antagonist looked like an Apache warrior as she peered down at us with the sun over her head: the prominence of her bosom made it appear that her arms were perpetually folded across her chest, and the makeup she had on begged to be compared to war paint.

The girls returned to the rear seat of the truck, picked up their smoking supplies and handbags, and left us forever. I watched them stand by the side of the road opposite the service station for about half an hour before they got a ride with two gentlemen in an old blue convertible. Just after the girls left, my father emerged from under the truck for the last time. He drove the vehicle forward and back, pausing to check his work on the driveshaft in each of several positions. At last he was satisfied that the repair was finished, and washed up his face and hands in the men's room. This was about two o'clock. For the remainder of the afternoon, he and I took turns looking in opposite directions down the road for signs of Mr. Poupolatos' car. My father proved to have less endurance at this game than I, and through the late afternoon and early evening he was either looking at the road map or taking short naps.

You can see that my father and I made the mistake of anticipating Maryann's arrival far too much. This may go a long way toward explaining why, when she did show up at eight o'clock that evening, we were disappointed with her.

"You got it fixed, did you?" she said over the din of the radio. She was sitting in Mr. Poupolatos' car, speaking to us through an open window. "We saw George's brother and ordered the parts. They're going to be on the bus tomorrow morning. George said we could stay in his motel tonight. He's going to have a party for us."

Maryann opened the door of the Poupolatos automobile and climbed out. "Do you know how George got started in flying?" she asked us. "When he was fifteen, he got this idea to write to Greek churches all over the country and ask people to send him airplane parts. He got his engine from Portland and one of his landing wheels from Florida. People in the church sent all the parts to him. And he built his first airplane." Maryann ran a comb through her hair and then handed the comb back to Mr. Poupolatos.

"Tomorrow he's going to take me for a ride in his airplane," she said. "That's the new one, not the one he built."

My father watched the taillights of automobiles and trucks disappear around a distant turning of the road while Maryann was speaking. When she was finished, he took her hand and walked her off to the other side of the truck. The shadows of their legs and feet conferred in whispers. Mr. Poupolatos slouched in the dome-lit interior of his car, which had been emptied of its earlier contents of family and refilled, via a radio station in Little Rock, with Frank Sinatra. My father and Maryann raised their voices at each other. They stamped, like a duet in a parade, to the door of Maryann's trailer. Suitcases belonging to my father and myself were thrown out. Maryann's travel blanket and a box of Kleenex were picked from the cab of the truck.

All of our belongings were segregated. At the end, oh bitter to remember, Maryann's trailer was unhitched from the ball of our truck and her brake-light wires were pulled out.

All this was done amid a certain amount of hysterical crying, in which Mr. Poupolatos did not participate noticeably. Mr. Poupolatos stayed in his car, but performed his part in the unhitching operation by turning on his headlights at an appropriate moment.

How the traffic had increased on the road after sundown! Even after my father and I had slammed the doors on the truck and driven to the edge of the highway, we were obliged to stop there for an extremely long time, looking far down the road for the break in traffic that would let us out. At first my father raced the engine in his impatience, then he subsided into a rubbernecked vigil. But instead of the break in traffic he was pretending to be looking for, what should appear at the window on my father's side but Maryann: not a ghost Maryann, or an imagined Maryann, or even a remembered Maryann, but a real Maryann. She was weeping.

"Wait," she said, really quite unnecessarily. We had waited for her all afternoon without once being asked.

chapter nine

WHEN WE FIRST ARRIVED in Los Alamos, I remember being
enormously disappointed. I may have felt this way in sympathy with Maryann, who developed a poor opinion of the place
in a short time, although it's true that some aspects of Los
Alamos left me worse off than she was.

Had my father misrepresented Los Alamos to us? I hardly
think so. In Tulsa he told us about the herds of wild antelope
which people there saw every day as moving patches of color
far out on the desert, identifiable only by the plumes of dust
they raised when they ran. In Oklahoma City he told us about
the daylong sunshine we would have in the rare, mile-high air.
We would pick the strawberries which littered the sides of
nearby Guaje Mountain. In Amarillo, the three of us pasted
our New Mexico map down on the coffee stains of a diner and
enjoyed the names of the towns near our new home: Santa Fe,
Albuquerque, Grants, Gallup. My father pointed out the
Pecos River. In Tucumcari we sent Maryann's mother and
father a postcard with a glossy print of Route 66 lined with

Christmas decorations. We passed through some of the afternoon thundershowers he had told us about, with their tails of purple rain which evaporate before they hit the ground. As we drove under one I saw the rain falling above us, but we never got wet.

So what was there about Los Alamos that disappointed us? Maryann and I should have suspected what it was when we checked in with the liaison office in Santa Fe. My father stopped the truck in front of what appeared to be an ordinary house except for the enormous piles of military and scientific equipment stacked about the door. Military tents were pitched in the front yard area, each one containing either soldiers or supplies. While my father was inside signing forms or whatever, a dust-covered sedan with five women in it drove up behind our truck. The women all got out and walked to the door of the liaison office. Each of them was carrying something: one bore a hammer, two others were carrying cloth sacks which looked as though they might be made out of men's socks, and the remainder carried soiled babies' diapers. When the women reached the door of the liaison office, instead of entering they went to work nailing these various burdens all around the outside of the building. Many of them chalked large signs on the siding.

"What do those signs say?" I whispered to Maryann.

"I can't read all of them," she said. "They have German words in them. But the two on the left say 'Bad Meat' and 'No Water.'"

One of the women who had brought her diapers in a pail was now drawing the same pail full of water at a spigot. When the pail was full, she threw its entire contents against the side of the building where the diapers were pinned, making reddish-brown torrents rush out. The women gathered up their tools and drove away.

My father came out carrying various papers and envelopes. He seemed distracted and bewildered by the mess which was posted on the front of the liaison office. He glanced back over his shoulder at it several times before reaching us.

"Was that there when I went in?" he asked Maryann.

"Some women delivered it," she said, "while you were inside."

My father must have felt some sort of obligation to explain what we had seen to us, but the embarrassing fact was that we had seen it and he hadn't. "Those must have been some of the scientists' wives," he said. "Did you meet any of them?"

"They were in a hurry," Maryann said.

"Oh, well," my father said, starting the engine, "there'll be time enough for introductions when we get to the mesa."

Maryann and I were surprised that even though we had reached Santa Fe, Los Alamos still lay twenty-five hot, dusty miles away. My father engaged four-wheel drive for most of the trip along the rutted road. Mailboxes on the other side of the drainage ditch had Spanish names on them. We could see across the flatlands for miles to the mesas all around with their sheer sides and level tops. A flimsy wooden railroad trestle led us across the Rio Grande, which shocked me by being a muddy trickle, to the base of the 7300-foot-high Parajito Plateau, the mesa upon which Los Alamos was being built. Before we had mounted this twisting road very far, we passed some stray cows lying on their stomachs under piñon trees.

"Look," said Maryann. "Mountain lie-ons." She broke me up. I laughed until it seemed I was placing my pants in danger.

This was late summer in the great spaces of the Southwest. The greasewood and sage of our dusty desert ride were extremely pale in color, as if they were trying to hide in the desert. The ranches we had passed and their tall plumage of cottonwoods huddling around steel windmills looked as if they had no plans for winter. Chipmunks idled in the sun. Prairie dogs' holes dotted the desert, making snake-traps which my father had warned me to keep my hands out of. Desert roses were so bold as to scrape the side of our truck as we climbed the twisting road.

"Nelson Nachtigall told me a hairy story about this road," my father said. "He was driving a pick-up down one day and the accelerator stuck. He said he went around a couple of these hairpin turns on two wheels before he finally went off the road. The truck rolled over but it didn't burn. I guess he was pretty lucky."

"He went off the road? *This* road?" Maryann said. I understood what she was talking about. The road we were driving on dropped off steeply on one side; the other side was a sheer wall.

"He said some trees kept him from falling off the mesa," my father said. The trees we were now passing were mostly lissom aspens, their dull-gold leaves tiny discs against the blue sky. I really didn't see how these or their runty associates, the red oak scrubs, could do much of a job restraining Nachtigall and his pick-up. A few blue-black pines gave the only stalwart indications on the slope.

The road grader had provided a shallow drainage ditch on the uphill side of the road, and yellow flowers grew here. The flowers were covered with dust; passed by, it would seem, by too many scientists' cars in too much of a hurry. Whenever the hood of our truck curved out over a vista of the desert floor and the blue-gray rock mountains in the distance, I was reminded how wild this place was.

In one pulling-over place my father stopped the truck on a bed of pine needles and let the engine idle with his hand brake on while he worked under the hood. When he was through, he slammed the hood down and took his place in the cab again.

"What did you do?" Maryann asked him.

"I leaned out the mixture a little," my father said. "It was starting to run rough at this high altitude. I should probably change the spark, too, but I guess that can wait until we get to the top." Behind us the great, rough slopes were gold with aspen and dark blue with spruce. We saw the Rio Grande, which we had crossed with so little celebration, as a crumpled crack in the desert. The occasional dead tree was having its top bleached by the sun.

As we neared the top of the mesa, the foliage became smaller and less impressive. Mountain grass, sharp-sided and hugging the center of the two ruts, became the highest-standing thing. Abruptly we came up a final stretch of gravelly grade and there was Los Alamos.

"Brother," Maryann said. "Let's go home." I didn't blame her. It was unimaginably ugly, even by the standards of Happy Valley. The central landmark of the town was its water tower, which stood above everything else. On the highest ground were the log buildings of the boys' school which had been here before the atomic project had ever been conceived. Directly before us was the tent and trailer city which we had been told would only be temporary until houses could be built. The central street even had a name: Trinity Avenue. To the west was the fenced-off Technical Area, whose buildings and shops we had interrupted in the midst of construction.

My father had told us that we would be living in one of the log houses of the old Los Alamos Ranch School for Boys, and this was both to Maryann's satisfaction and my own, when we saw what the people in the tent and trailer city were putting up with. None of the unpaved streets had names. Every one of the tents and trailers, plus what few temporary buildings existed, were painted green. Clothes were strung on lines stretched between the trailers, and portable outdoor toilets were lined up between the dwellings. A single consolation to the inhabitants was their view: to the east lay the Sangre de Cristo range, and to the west were the Jemez mountains.

"Who has to live here?" I asked my father.

"Most everyone lives here," my father said. "All the military and technicians' families, at least. We're lucky, actually, that we're not a military family right now; the original plan was for everyone working on this project, scientists included, to be commissioned as officers."

"Jesus," Maryann said. "It must be swell being a military family."

We left the ghetto of stovepipe chimneys and community washtubs behind. My father stopped the truck in front of a three-story log structure with a wide porch and a sign on it which said "Fuller Lodge." He led us inside. The screen door led into a large front room with a stone fireplace and hickory furniture. The floor was made out of wide pine boards and had a high gloss. There were several windows in the room but none of them seemed to be doing its job properly; the room was dark and cool even though it was only mid-afternoon. Many people were standing around the room posing for us, a large number sitting down in the hickory chairs, but the majority standing at a bar where an attendant in a white bar jacket was mixing drinks.

"Harold MacLaurin's here!" shouted someone, and in a moment nearly the entire group was pumping my father's hand. They asked him how his trip had been. "Still got that trail dust on your clothes, I see," they kept saying. "Somebody show him his house and let him get that *trail dust* off his clothes."

One of the scientists there was Nelson Nachtigall, who appointed himself to show us our house. Nelse was with a sleepy-eyed blond girl named Fred who, it was explained, worked in an Albuquerque art supply shop and was just visiting for a few days. Nelse and Fred bottoms-upped their drinks and came blinking outside with us into the sun.

Our house had been one of the faculty houses of the Los Alamos Ranch School. It had four rooms, all on one floor, including an inside bathroom and a bathtub.

"The people who live down in the tent city call this part of town 'Bathtub Row,'" Nelse explained. "All they have down there are those outside showers. You should hear their wives scream."

"This place is cherry," Maryann said, visibly pleased. We walked through the rooms, thumping the floor and walls with our heels and knuckles, testing everything. "This place is definitely cherry," Maryann said. We tried the faucet at the kitchen sink and not very much water came out. The fireplace in the living room had charred logs in it, and most of the ashtrays scattered around on the floor were full.

"I've been staying here until you came," Nelse said in the way of an explanation. "Don't worry, though," he added quickly. "I've been given a room at the bachelor dorms, so you won't be putting me out."

"Oh, I hope you'll *excuse* me," Fred said from one of the daybeds in the living room, where she was languidly reclining. "I just don't know what's the *matter* with me today, I feel so *tired*." Fred spread her sweet blond hair on the pillow and smiled absently. Her cowboy shirt hugged her narrow waist.

"I feel a little sleepy myself," Nelse said, yawning. "Fred and I drove up here from Albuquerque this morning. She had to work yesterday."

"It's such a bore," Fred said from the flowered bedspread, leaning up on one arm. "My job, I mean."

"What do you do?" asked Maryann, who was standing near the door. She had not been listening earlier to Nelse's explanation of Fred.

"I work in this art supply store. I'm only doing it temporarily, you know, between my regular jobs."

"What's your regular job?" Maryann asked.

"I was trained to be an Indian agent. Social work and all that. I graduated from the New Mexico Social Work School. But since the war started, the government hasn't been spending much money on the Indians, and I've been out of work."

"That's too bad," Maryann said.

"It's too bad for me, but it's worse for the Indians," Fred told us, sitting up. "They're really pitiful. You should see the holes they live in on the reservation. They have zero pride in themselves. It's really awful." Fred smiled again.

"What a shame," Maryann said.

Nelse helped my father bring in several boxes of our belongings from the back of our truck. While Fred rested on the daybed, Maryann and I emptied the ashtrays and swept the floor. Maryann even tried a little window cleaner on one of the six-paned front windows, with a great deal of success. I got a kick out of the way Maryann immediately organized things as they were brought inside.

"I know what we all need to wake ourselves up," Nelse said at the end of one of his trips. "An ankle-wetting."

"Yes!" came Fred's affirmation from the daybed.

"She likes to have her ankles wet," Nelse said to my father. "How about it, then?"

"Yes! Yes!" said Fred, removing her shoes and socks. Maryann stopped cleaning the stove and looked around. "How about you?" Fred asked her. "It's such a good time."

"Thanks just the same," Maryann said. "You go ahead." She returned to the scouring with an energy I had never seen her devote to housework. She was making such an effort to distinguish herself from the Fred image that she kept polishing the same place on the inside of the stove until it was ridiculous.

Nelse and Fred went outside on the patch of brown mountain grass which we used for a lawn, and Nelse turned the hose on Fred's bare feet. She screamed and pranced as he hosed her. My father watched from the door. "Are you sure you don't want to get in on this?" he asked Maryann.

"No, thank you, but you go ahead," she sang, her voice echoing from the interior of the oven. I could tell my father had been battling with himself over whether or not to confront Maryann with her own dismaying inconsistency. Could she possibly have any idea how she had been looking to other people since our departure from Oak Ridge? Were there any words to bring her to focus her inner mind on her outer self and see that whatever it was she had been disappointed in not finding in the world beyond her hometown; whatever it was that was making her act like a captured princess in a foreign court; whatever it was that was making a lovely young girl stick her head in an oven; was an illusion?

"You go ahead, you go ahead," my father said sarcastically, striding over to her. "It's only for fun, Maryann. Come off it, won't you?" He had meant to give her a chance to laugh at herself, but she didn't take it. She didn't even look up. She didn't speak more than a few sentences to any one of us for the rest of the day.

In the late afternoon, the military police came around and accused us of being prodigal with the water. Nelse turned the hose off and he and Fred devoted themselves to other romping sports on the lawn until nightfall. Maryann served us a cold supper at the kitchen table, and afterwards we played poker. Maryann played badly: it was obvious that either she wasn't trying or she hadn't learned properly from her libertine friends back home. My father may have felt like making a remark to this effect, but he stifled it. Maryann soon left the table and I was invited to fill her spot, but this signaled the doom of the game as I didn't know poker at all and had to be taught. I also had to be given back any pots which I lost, and this destroyed the competitive aspect of the playing.

The sharp, blue New Mexican night came down on us and left the lawn a dark shore around our house. When he was confident that the military police had been by on their rounds for the last time of the evening, Nelse attached the hose to the outside spigot again. All of us except Maryann sneaked out the door and carried the trickling hose around to the back of the house. Nelse was acting terribly peckery, putting his hand on Fred's bottom and all. We all shot each other with the water to some extent, but Fred and Nelse dominated the action. Fred took off her clothes, revealing a two-piece bathing suit which Nelse proceeded to wet down thoroughly. Fred held the hose over her head, making the trickling water come in a shiny rivulet down her blond hair, flowing off stiff wet points of it onto her shoulders and the white breasts which her sagging suit left nearly bare. Nelse abruptly turned the water on full force when Fred was attempting to drink from the hose. In spite of my callow age, as I watched Fred wetted down under the moonlight I felt my pants getting tighter and tighter.

"Like her, Timmy?" Nelse asked me. We were leaning against the back of the house, in a kind of sitting position with our knees up. How could he have known that I was interested in the sight Fred was putting on before us? He was just teasing me. It turned out he was teasing my father, too.

"I just love sex," he said to my father. "It's so lovely. I think about it all the time." He borrowed my father's pipe and sucked on it wildly, making the red eye in the bowl devour the wet Fred on the lawn.

Nelse and Fred spent that night in the cabin; we slept in our trailer for a last time. In the morning Nelse and Fred were gone. They left a note but it didn't say much of anything.

chapter ten

MARYANN, DR. ORR, MY FATHER AND I SPENT an afternoon
together on the desert shortly after our arrival at Los Alamos.
How unfortunate it is that one always has to have before him
the apprehension that his readers won't believe him. Perhaps
the requirement that a story must be believable is some member of an elegant set of literary checks and balances; nonetheless it is an encumbrance to one who has a true story and
desires to tell it forthright, exactly as it happened. Would
anyone believe me, for instance, if I were to describe our
truck parked on the desert floor, its radio on, its tailgate
down, and Maryann casting sharp shadows as she practiced
her dancing, sliding one hand along the tailgate-turned-
dancing-bar? Is it especially believable that Dr. Orr was perfectly visible to us, even though he was a quarter of a mile
away, bent over examining a red flowering plant? Do you see
my father and me, sitting side by side on a desert dune,
watching Maryann exercise and waiting for the sunset?

I was asking my father about the desert, and he was an-

71

swering me. He told me that sand gets more and more rounded as it blows about, eventually approaching a perfectly spherical shape which it then keeps, without further wearing, for millions of years.

About duststorms he said the following. High winds blow a mist of suspended dust and sand high into the air. When the mist clears, the heavier sand particles remain as a low, thick cloud. The air above is clear, and the heads of people (and of ostriches, which are built to survive duststorms) stick out of the cloud. The abrasive effect of the moving sand is greatest at ground level and diminishes to nothing a few feet off the ground. This is why rocks get carved at their bases and telephone poles are cut off neatly at the ground unless they are shielded by metal.

Maryann, wearing an MIT sweatshirt over her dancing tights, was perspiring even though the warmest part of the day was over. The trip to the desert had been her idea, and we suspected that she proposed it because she was self-conscious about exercising in Los Alamos, there being so little room in our cabin and no privacy outside. We alternately saw her reddening face and her ponytail hair as she sprang and bobbed, bumped and ground. From the open door of the truck cab, Benny Goodman squeaked into the desert. Strands of hair which worked their way out of Maryann's ponytail dampened themselves on the back of her neck to the swing beat of "One O'clock Jump" and "Sensation Rag." I tried to decide whether old Dr. Orr, who was now bent over a new plant in the distance, was bobbing with the music or merely shimmering in the layer of hot air above the sand. Dr. Orr straightened and walked toward us. His feet splashed through puddles apparent only to us, who watched him through a mirage. In one hand he carried the uprooted flowering plant, from which

72

clods of dirt kept falling into the imaginary wavelets. Mary-ann stopped dancing as he came within range of the more exalted of her kicks, and they spoke together with gestures involving the plant through six bars or more of "When My Baby Smiles at Me." Then Dr. Orr continued slowly up the side of the dune to the point where my father and I were perched, and sat down beside us. He hollowed out a little place in the sand and replanted his prize, tamping the roots all around with the tips of his fingers when he was finished.

"What on earth are we doing here?" he said, with the accent on *earth* as if he had forgotten it was sand we were seated in.

"We're watching Maryann dance," my father said.

"Now, yes, we're watching Maryann dance. But what shall we do this evening, and what tomorrow morning? Everyone in Los Alamos stays up so late at night, and they smoke so many cigarettes. They eat Velveeta cheese on crackers and they make terrible tea in their tubulated retorts. What makes them willing to work so hard for so long when the chances of making an atomic bomb are still small? It's like nothing I've seen before in science."

"Come now," my father said, tapping his foot in the sand to that incomparable Goodman sound.

"I mean it," Dr. Orr said. "For a thousand years, physicists have done their physics with bits of string, glass, paste, pipe cleaners and such. The man who felt he needed a lot of equipment went outdoors and watched the stars go by. Now what is it? Cockcroft-Walton particle accelerators, cyclotrons, secret laboratories in the desert, the American Army telling everyone what to do! I might have more freedom to do as I wished if I had stayed in Copenhagen."

My father didn't even raise an eyebrow at this. Maryann

went into a little war-dance routine, doing a step where she nearly touched her cheeks with her knees. The long shadows from the sun, which was nearly on the horizon, stretched Maryann's legs across the sand to some dark vanishing point.

"I'll tell you something, Harold," he went on. "I'll tell you what an ungodly time I had getting here. First, I got a letter, before the Germans even came, from Ferrini. Did I want to come spend the summer with him? For what foolish reason, I wrote him. But before I could even post my letter, I got a form from your State Department, an application for an immigrant visa. So Ferrini was in your country and I didn't even know this! The next week, a young lady arrived at my laboratories. By then, the Germans were everywhere. This young lady took out of her bag a hypodermic needle and shot me in the arm. 'Now we can go to America,' she said. 'Everyone who comes to America has to be immunized.' Then she sealed me up inside of a beer keg, slipped my only grandchild into her shopping bag, and we were off in an airplane. 'Not to worry,' she said. 'If we're attacked by the Germans, we'll parachute you into the ocean.' Even so, she made me come out of the barrel when she found I hadn't filled out my immigration papers and landing card. 'You get through customs so much faster if this is all done beforehand,' she said."

My father smiled at Maryann once when she stopped to let the people at the radio studio change records. "Bravo," he said with his lips. Dr. Orr, patting the roots of his plant with the tips of his fingers, must have accidentally stuck himself with a thorn of nostalgia. "In Copenhagen, from the front windows of my home where I also have my laboratory, I often watch the sun setting, as we are doing now. But with one important difference, Harold. My front windows face to the east, and when the sun is setting, I see the dark sky before anyone

74

else, growing from a ribbon into a patch above the houses. I watch the sun setting as a reflection in the windows of my neighbors. Sometimes I see several red suns at once, depending on how the windows are turned."

Orr smoothed back what remained of his white hair and pointed north into the desert. "Up there, on the Los Alamos mesa, I suspect it's quite impossible to see the sun setting by reflections. The design of the place is quite wrong for such things; what one needs is a city with a great deal of glass in it. I suspect, although I once thought I knew physics intimately, that it has moved away from me, moved away from Copenhagen: that the purpose of all this has been to force anyone who wishes to see the sun go down to come to the American desert and look at it directly."

Dr. Orr's presence in Los Alamos was regarded by nearly every member of the community as somehow vaguely auspicious. The scientists who arrived on the mesa top, each one having been procured through some furtive interview to engage in work which he knew only as "highly secret" and "vital to the war," were at once calmed and elated to learn of Dr. Orr's residence there. Dr. Orr's reputation was as great as that of any living physicist; his humility and sense of fair play merely increased his stature, like an appropriate crown. In the company of junior men, he would wear his white "top secret" security clearance badge on the inside lapel of his jacket, where it could not cause the wearers of the green and red lower clearances the usual anxiety of comparison. ("Look at it this way," said one of my father's friends with whom I have since talked about these badges. "If you were a woman with no build at all, would you want to stand next to Jane Russell in the showers?")

It was nearly dark when we stopped the truck before a

small shallow pond at the edge of the desert. Maryann and Dr. Orr rushed out of the cab down to the water, where they splashed around looking for frogs. My father and I obliged them by driving the truck to various places at the water's edge, shining the headlights into the water to their directions. Maryann's good legs shone luminously in the beams, as did Dr. Orr's white hair. Maryann often had her hands on her hips, shifting her weight from one foot to the other. She carried her shoes in one hand.

In the privacy of the cab, I asked my father, "There's nothing in the water that will hurt them?"

"I wouldn't think so, Tim," he said. "Frogs, insects, and a few freshwater shrimp. There are probably shrimp eggs in the hardened mud for miles around this area. They may have to wait for a hundred years for enough rain water to collect over their particular spot in the desert to hatch out. In past ages, this whole plain has been the floor of a lake."

I was momentarily afraid some shrimp might wiggle between Maryann's toes on the muddy bottom. Her back was still to us, her loosely blowing sweatshirt sometimes flattening against her. Dr. Orr came out of the water first, with Maryann following.

"I need a jar with a top on it," Dr. Orr said when he reached us. My father gave him our pickle jar, after removing the last pickle and wrapping it in a napkin. Dr. Orr emptied the remaining brine from the jar, swabbed the inside with another napkin, and bounced back to the pond. Maryann didn't get into the cab immediately. She stood outside eating the pickle my father had saved for her, staring out into the dark desert. Some clouds fooled with the moon and then left it alone.

"I don't feel like going back to the mesa now," she said.

"There are a lot of things I don't feel like doing," my father said, "but I do them because I have to."

"You'd be amazed," Maryann said, "at the things I don't have to do."

chapter eleven

On a recent occasion when my father and I were working together repairing the roof on the barn, I was pleased to find him in a mood willing to talk about the old days in physics. He usually discourages me from being nostalgic about the atomic bomb project: his disposition against discussing the Los Alamos years may be a hangover from the ordeal of the security scandals of the 1950's when he was so often pressured to make statements about his friends which he feared might be used later as evidence against them. It's an unusual day when I can get my father really to open up and talk to me about what he was doing during the war.

Our roofing job requires us to carry fifty-pound bales of asphalt shingles up a ladder to the roof. My father enjoys this kind of heavy work even today, and works without a shirt whenever there is an opportunity. I won't say that he was making a contest of carrying shingles up the ladder, but by the end of the morning, I was very close to exhaustion and my pile still hadn't matched his. The bright reflection from his wristwatch cut back and forth in the corner of my eye as he hammered: he might have been using a scythe. From the roof, we could see the flat fields all around and the woods a little distant. The dirt farm road running past our white house stretched off straight before us, disappearing near the woods as a hill carried it downwards.

My father and I had our lunch under a tree near the barn. "I'm not sure I can tell you anything you don't already know, Tim," he said. "You have my two *Journal of Fluid Mechanics* papers here; I think they describe most of what came out of my war research."

Both of his papers were published in the same blue-bound volume I had carried outside with the picnic basket. I had made my way through each of the papers several times before, but many points of the analysis remained a puzzle to me. The first of the two papers, an editorial note explained, was written in 1943, but had not been published until 1950, when it had been declassified. This first paper explained how the author had been asked to think about the effects of a unique kind of explosion: namely one which took place in a real atmosphere when a very large quantity of energy was suddenly released at a point. The author stipulated that at the time he developed the mathematical model for this energy explosion, every aspect of the problem was purely hypothetical since no such event had ever happened on the earth before, and there was therefore no body of experimental evidence to suggest an appropriate direction for the analysis.

He had been asked, the author went on, to decide how effective this energy explosion would be as a blast producer in comparison with the blast effects of a chemical bomb of similar energy. The difference between the two explosions would be fundamentally that the chemical explosion would release a quantity of gas into the atmosphere which would expand in time like a solid sphere, a situation which is not terribly difficult to analyze using classical one-dimensional gas dynamics. But for the energy explosion, one would have to know how the release of energy in the form of light, heat, and other types of radiation would make use of the surrounding atmosphere as the driving gas for the expanding shock wave.

The author started by writing the conservation equations for mass, momentum, and energy including heat addition, assuming that pressure, density, and radial velocity were all functions of radial distance and time only. Then the author introduced assumed similarity forms for the independent variables. The special form of these variables made me think that the author knew the answer to the problem before he started it.

"What made you think of just these expressions?" I asked my father. "They aren't at all obvious to me. I never would have guessed the forms you assume here."

"It isn't as arbitrary as you might think, Tim," he said. "I didn't have to present these forms at the beginning; I could have chosen a general expression for each of the quantities and evaluated the exponents at the end of the analysis."

I turned to the closing pages of the paper to see if he was right. It still seemed a little muddled. "Then what is it you do here?" I asked him. "You change variables to this dimensionless radial coordinate?"

"Yes," he said.

He flipped through the pages on my lap and showed me the log-log plot of shock radius versus time in the second paper, along with several photographs of the atomic fireball growing on the desert floor. Even after all these years, the photographs still shock me. The fireball is so big.

"This may seem a little magical to you, but I think you'll see how it occurred to me if you follow through the more rigorous argument I've given in the second paper. I wanted to get a set of dimensionless ordinary differential equations involving my arbitrary functions to replace the equations of motion. Then for boundary conditions I just took the Rankine-Hugoniot relations in their strong shock form. If you put these together you get the specific values the arbitrary functions take on for a perfect gas, and you can see they're all constants."

I looked where he was pointing and saw that it was true. The way he had used his intuition to lead his mathematics was nothing less than elegant. I read on through his papers in silence for about a quarter of an hour while he got up and walked around. In the second paper he had written integral expressions for the total kinetic and potential energy enclosed within the shock wave and shown how a particular constant mentioned earlier could be derived in terms of these energies. Then the total energy released by the explosion bore a simple power-law relation to the rate of propagation of the blast wave at any time. He explained how it would be possible to know the total energy released by an atomic bomb simply by taking a picture of it at a given time after its detonation, or by taking two pictures separated by a known time interval.

"This is fantastic," I told him when he came back. "This part where you get the energy yield from a measurement of the rate of growth of the fireball."

"Frisky liked that," my father said. "You remember Frisky Sandeman, the scientific director at Los Alamos?"

"Sure," I said. "I remember him. He was pleased when you did this derivation?"

"I don't think he was pleased until after the test, when

those similarity forms I assumed turned out to be right. You see in the second paper where I predict that the explosion is likely to be only about half as effective a blast producer as the chemical bomb? He was surprised at that." My father stood up, found a package of cigarettes in his back pocket, and sat down again. "But it turned out to be true," he said finally. "And it was just one of Frisky's surprises. He's had a lot of them since the end of the project. Perhaps we all have."

I let him take his time in beginning to tell me what he meant by this. He didn't seem to be ready to start by himself, so I asked him, "What do you mean by surprises?"

"Well," he said, sort of sighing, "I wonder if I can tell you. We were all young when we started the Manhattan project. I was thirty-six, Richie Mundi and Nelse Nachtigall were younger. Nearly all of us were either youngsters or people like Orr and Ferrini, who were grand old men even then. Many of us hadn't even finished our degrees; it was necessary to take people out of graduate school to work on the project." He crossed his legs and pulled a little at one trouser leg. "Los Alamos was a very special time for us," he said. "Everyone had suddenly to show, in a very short time, the very best that his science could do. The ones of us who had been trained in the pure sciences, where we were accustomed to having as long as we wanted to explore every interesting alley of a new idea before we did much of anything, all at once found ourselves having to work with engineers who had a specific job they wanted to do *now*. And by God, we had to do that job *now*. So we worked long hours, and even though we worked closely together, we were lonely in our research because it meant so much to us."

I hadn't been able to listen to my father until this last, this bit about the loneliness on research. It represented somehow an admission of what we don't admit, the statement of a condition we only live in and never state. The loneliness of research. It's what I worked so hard to learn in school, and never learned. I seek it and it seeks me. It waits for me in the world outside our farm, and I shall go to it again when I leave here, and give it my health. I look forward to it, yet I fear it.

"I'm interested in that," I told my father. "I'm interested in how you all felt when you were inventing the atomic bomb."

"We felt . . ." my father said, "rushed, but I suppose we weren't unhappy. We had each other's fellowship and the rhythm of our jobs to carry us forward. We just did things from day to day. In the beginning the Army supported us and never interfered with us. We stayed up all night sometimes, talking and thinking about the new vistas in the physical sciences we seemed to be approaching. It seemed to us that although our country was at war, and our days were caught up in the life of that war, the things we were doing in our evenings were eternal. That may be why my friends at Brookhaven are nostalgic and want to talk about those old days so much. They say they miss the times at the beginning of the project when we used to have all-night bull sessions with people like Ferrini and Orr. They moan and say, 'Oh, look at the distractions and irrelevance we have to put up with in dealing with the military today; wasn't it wonderful when we lived up there in our ivory towers?' "

"But you don't feel that way?" I asked him.

"Aw, hell, I know what they're talking about," my father said. "There really was something good there. But whether we actually did those good things or just thought about them isn't clear to me any more. I can remember how nice it was to leave the technical compound at the end of a day and spend an evening on Ferrini's front porch drinking sours and philosophizing about physics. Whether any of us admitted it or not, we were all grateful to the circumstances of the world for having put us together and having separated us from the trouble of supporting our own work. It was the first time, really, that such a thing had ever happened. The Army more or less just said, 'Look, you guys go ahead and do whatever you want; we trust you and we're paying.' There were inconveniences about being so far away from Chicago or Cambridge or Berkeley or wherever we came from, but the real truth was that we were having a ball."

"And now you think this was an irresponsible way to have behaved?" I asked him. He had crossed his legs and was holding one ankle with both hands as if it were the tiller of an imaginary boat in which he and I were sailing, who knows where.

"It didn't seem irresponsible at the time," he said. "You've got to remember that none of us could see into the future: we didn't know that the Germans had given up their atomic bomb project. In fact, the British scientists in the group really expected the Germans to drop an atomic bomb on London at any moment."

I looked at my father holding his leg in the greenness under our shade tree and was momentarily terrified that he might be getting ready to die: might be preparing me for his death; might be apologizing to me; might be explaining to me.

"Irresponsible?" he said. "None of us felt irresponsible in 1943. But so much has happened since then . . ." He looked at me. "Maryann is gone, so much of our original idealism is compromised, your illness . . ." He looked at me again and I had this horror that perhaps the sight of me was making him nauseated.

He caught my eye and smiled for a moment; he needn't have: I know he wishes me well. This has always been between us. It has always been a comfort to me. I have never doubted it. He wishes me well.

"You've forgotten Maryann?" I asked him. He tugged on his trouser cuff and folded it between his first two fingers again and again.

"No," he said. "I haven't forgotten her. Although, to be truthful, you seem to remember more about her than I do. Sometimes I remember so little about her that she might never have existed."

"She existed when you wrote the first of these papers," I said, holding the blue-bound volume. "When you had that inspiration that let you see your way through to the physical design. She was with us then."

"Yes," he said. "I suppose you're right."

chapter twelve

ONE EVENING DURING THE FIRST YEAR we were at Los Alamos, Dr. Sandeman declared that it was his birthday and he wanted to drive to Santa Fe and eat Mexican food. The military commandant of the project, General Windkessel, disapproved of night trips away from the mesa, but everyone understood this to be part of his ridiculous safety fetish about the dangerous mountain road, and disobeyed him.

This isn't to say that people regarded the trip to Santa Fe casually. Before you could begin the hazards of the mountain road after dark, it was necessary to strike an agreement with Sergeant Forbes, the old military policeman at the guardhouse by the main gate. The agreement usually involved five dollars, and you had to tell Forbes exactly when you would be back, so that he could be awake to open the gate for you.

At dusk the road could be counted on to be lovely, since the aspen trunks would divide the red fatness of the sun like a venetian blind, making marvelous effects on the uneven pine-needle roadbed. But when the last light of the sun was gone, the moonlight and starlight which might have taken its place were shut out by thick fir branches over the turning road, creating a rich and complete darkness. People would proceed carefully, some of them removing the slit masking from their headlights, until they gained the open country at the foot of the mesa.

In Santa Fe, Sandeman and his guests ate at La Casita, which you have to ask people directions to, even if you've been there several times, as Sandeman had. It's necessary to go through someone's pepper garden, stepping on stepping-stones, in order to get there. Sandeman ordered green pepper enchiladas. He cut them up and ate them with the six-inch knife he kept in a sheath at his belt, drinking gallons of water and wiping his knife often on his napkin. He explained that the La Casita pepper juice was hard on his knife and would make it dull after only one meal if he didn't take care to clean it off after he used it. Before he finished his last enchilada his lips were a bright pink.

After the meal, Nelse Nachtigall challenged Sandeman to a round on the pinball machine. This instrument was extremely old. Its case was cracked mahogany and its legs were ornate cast iron. The name of the game was "Love," and painted around each of the posts the ball might have hit on its way back to the chute was a beautiful girl dressed in flapper clothes, whose name — Minnie, Fran, Alice — was painted beside her face. Some of the girls wore bathing suits and others were dressed in formal gowns. Sandeman and Nachtigall were amused by their game, but not by Minnie, Fran, or Alice. They were amused by the similarity of the spring-operated ball launching mechanism to the detonation gun they were presently considering on the mesa. Assuming the exchange of spring for a little charge of gunpowder, they saw that here before them was a prototype of the best idea they had had yet for assembling the critical mass of fissionable materials. And it couldn't be expected to work much better than this game of Love.

Meanwhile my father and Maryann, the other two guests on the birthday trip, lingered at their table over iced tea. A man in Eastern clothing at a table behind them was speaking in a loud voice to his friend.

"I think I understand love as a marketplace as well as anyone I know," this man was saying. "I think I understand sex and money as negotiables which wives and husbands exchange. No one expects something for nothing, and in order for business to go on, no one hoards his fortune. It's against the rules. It dries up the commerce.

"Last year at Christmas we had a little recession at our house. It was tight money and tight ass for a while. My wife knows I like to bend it with our friends on New Year's Eve, but for a sort of punishment she turns down the invitation to the party I wanted to go to. 'No, thank you,' she says. 'We're all a little under the weather over here and we wouldn't want to give you our colds. But thank you just the same. I always feel just as grateful, when someone invites me somewhere but I can't come, as if I had gone and had a good time.'

"The next day she accepts an invitation from her ugly sister and my fathead brother-in-law to have New Year's Eve dinner at an expensive restaurant in town. At the dinner I'm expected to pick up the tab because everyone knows I make so much more money than my brother-in-law. The cashier short-changes me and wishes me a Happy New Year. Then we go to their house where we watch them play with their cat for a couple of hours. They throw a piece of paper up in the air and their cat jumps for it. They jump their cat until he won't jump any more, and then we go home.

"So there we are getting ready for bed, and I make a little move for her, and right away she says, 'don't.' Thereupon I explain it to her, about how the meal cost me fifty bucks, I can't stand her sister and her husband, I missed my party, but I did it all for her and now I figure she owes me a fuck. She actually had to have this all explained to her. Life would be so much simpler if people wouldn't order things they didn't want to pay for."

Sandeman and Nachtigall played the pinball machine until it broke down. Justi, the owner of La Casita, turned the machine on its back and took the bottom off. Sandeman and Nachtigall squatted around and gave advice while Justi repaired it. In this undignified position, the Love machine looked like a dead steer with its four hooves in the air. When it was working again, Sandeman and Nachtigall offered to buy it.

"What do you want with it?" Justi asked them.

"We want to make an atomic bomb out of it," Nachtigall said. This made a dark look come across Sandeman's face, and he glanced around to see who was listening. By this time the strangers had gone.

Justi couldn't be made to believe that their offer was serious. He just laughed them off and took their money for the enchiladas. Sandeman had forgotten his wallet and had to borrow from Dr. Nachtigall. He could be counted on to have forgotten his wallet in situations like this, although he always paid his debts promptly. People who traveled with him would just expect that he wouldn't have his wallet with him, and they'd carry extra money for his use. Still, they would let him go through the whole pocket-patting thing in front of the cash register every time, perhaps with the plan that the embarrassment might provoke him to change his habit.

Driving up the mesa road in the dark was something Sandeman should have given his full attention to. Even if one's mind couldn't be kept on the hairpin turns and narrow ruts, there were other matters: a light airplane had crashed somewhere near the mesa road years earlier and had never been found. Each time the headlights swerved out into the darkness of trees at a sharp turn, there was the possibility of their being reflected by lost, dead eyes hanging upside down from their seat belts. From episodes of very deep darkness, the car passed onto open, rocky ledges where the road had been made with dynamite, and even as the rear wheels skidded and bumped over places where the footing was marginal and the drop was potentially hundreds of feet, Sandeman and Nachtigall in the front seat talked on about bomb physics.

When they reached the guardhouse, they found Forbes had forgotten to leave the gate open. He had also forgotten to leave the lights on, making the place look deserted. Sandeman got out and called, but no one came. He rattled the gate. Eventually he came back to the car and beeped the horn. This brought a response: all the exterior lights came on and a young, slim MP, not Forbes, came out.

The MP wanted to see ID's. Sandeman said that wouldn't be necessary, Forbes had already taken the bribe and the time they were returning and the whole thing. The MP said Forbes was off duty and he wanted ID's from everybody. And a dollar from everybody, too, Sandeman thought out loud. He went on about this, saying that he wasn't about to pay five dollars to get out and another five dollars to get back in. My father,

Dr. Nachtigall, and Maryann each showed their ID's, Maryann's receiving more attention and Maryann herself a familiar look. Sandeman admitted that he didn't have his wallet with him, but he said he would look in his pockets for something else. When he opened his jacket, the enchilada knife bobbed free at his belt.

"No you don't, cocksucker," the MP said, and smashed Sandeman in the face with his rifle butt, sending a bright red jet down the front of his suit. Other soldiers came to the MP's aid. They took Sandeman's knife and pushed him into a detention cell. He was stripped nude and locked in. His clothes were thrown in a corner of the guardhouse.

"Hey, you knocked a couple of his teeth out, Mal," one of the soldiers said.

"That's too bad," Mal told him.

"Are you going to keep him in there all night?" Dr. Nachtigall asked.

"You bet the fucking suck I am," the MP said. "Until I find out who the fucker is. Fucking tries to pull a knife on me. He's lucky I didn't kill him. If the fucker had reached for my weapon, I'd have killed him."

Sandeman could be heard moaning in his detention cell.

"I can tell you who he is," Dr. Nachtigall said.

"You can tell me nothing, civilian mouth," Mal said. "You can get in your vehicle and get out of here before I fuck you up the way I did fuck-face there."

Nachtigall drove Maryann and my father to their cabin, and then went looking for General Windkessel.

If this had been a fine day and one was sitting in one's office making progress with calculations or theory, Windkessel would not be hard to find. One would have a right to expect that Windkessel would show up with a visitor who needed a tour, a household appliance which needed a repair, or an Army reminiscence which needed to be listened to. Windkessel had required a promotion from lieutenant colonel to general and a great deal of flattery to be induced to take this command. It had taken him only a short period of familiarization to discover that the scientists were a lazy bunch of lie-abouts; in explaining their syndrome of superiority and carelessness of their persons he had come to rely on analogy with a group every military man has met: the sons of the rich and politically powerful. Windkessel's one great cause was that the scientists all be made junior officers so that they would have an opportunity to rise earlier. He disliked the scientists for the very things — curiosity, indifference to political and ideological fundamentalism, jealousy of personal freedom — which made them scientists. He disliked Sandeman because he was a scientist, because he had responsibility for the scientists on the mesa, and because he let them get away with hell.

At this time, which was only late evening, Windkessel might have been found in his office at staff headquarters, in one of the staff headquarters latrines, or in his rooms in the Fuller Lodge, and Nachtigall looked in all these places without success. At the Lodge, Nachtigall succeeded in raising Windkessel's aide, a youthful soldier with bad skin who had been cleaning his rifle without any pants on. He hid behind a door, leaning into the crack to answer Nachtigall's questions. He gave Nachtigall directions to one of the trailers parked in the trailer city on the lower part of the mesa, but warned him that it had better be a matter of paramount importance for Windkessel to be disturbed there. Nachtigall assured him that it was.

The trailer Nachtigall found at the end of the directions was not at all like the one Maryann had been given to live in at Oak Ridge, but was long, wide, covered with a galvanized steel skin and fitted with louvered windows and screens. Nachtigall found the front door but no bell or knocker, so improvised with his knuckles. He knocked several times, and after a while a woman and a man came to the door in bathrobes. The man wasn't General Windkessel. When Nachtigall explained that he had come to see the general about an urgent matter, Windkessel appeared and said, "What urgent matter?" Nachtigall told him the story.

"That's rich," Windkessel said. He was a heavy man with those thick Arabian features which make you think of somebody T. E. Lawrence might have bought a horse from before he set off across the Sahara. "You mean my people have Sandeman ballacky bare-ass in a detention cell right now? What a sight. That's better than anything going on here. I'm tempted to come down and have a look."

Windkessel looked at his watch. "Say," he said, "I'm going to be tied up here until morning. Let's let old Göttingen-Berkeley stay down there until reveille, shall we? I'll issue orders for his release when I get to my quarters. You can go pick him up any time after seven."

"You're not going to get him out before morning?" Dr. Nachtigall asked.

"That's it, that's exactly it," Windkessel said. "I'm not going to get him out before morning." He closed the door and went back to his hosts.

But all this while Sandeman, alone in his cage, was drifting upward. A tooth had fallen out of his gums and he held this in his hand as if it were going to have to pay his fare somewhere. He was seated on a dirt floor with his back against a cinder block wall, but sometimes when the room lurched he had to catch his balance with his free hand. In rising into the em-

94

pyrean he was also rising into cosmic thoughtfulness, and his fortune was that it was the very fragile thoughtfulness which no one who lives on earth can save for himself for long: there are interruptions. Sandeman was rising for a while through ever-cooler layers of summer night air, leaving below him a country town on the green land from which the sounds of children playing could be heard. He rose through the smoke of campfires and the dust of Western landscapes until a special cleanness began at the base of the stratosphere. From the moment the horizon began to curve below him he rose faster, and on leaving the planets below and coming within range of the closer stars, took up a course on the Russell Diagram midway between the spectral classes and luminosity axes. "Oh, Be A Fine Girl, Kiss Me Right Now . . . Smack." Our sun, in spectral class G, was for an hour of his flight still the nearest heavenly body, with Sirius, in the main sequence, faintly visible. But he was lifting in a direction away from the carbon-nitrogen cycle stars, toward the red giants: Capella A sailed into view and disappeared as majestically as a religious holiday floating on the days of the calendar. His course took him midway into the cepheid variables, a group which seemed to know the tricks fog knows of thinning itself to become invisible when you come near. In the very center of the cepheid variables, Delta Cephei lay pulsing rhythmically in and out, its diameters heaving larger and smaller upon one another like a lung breathing. And here Sandeman lost consciousness.

The next morning Dr. Nachtigall transported Sandeman to the infirmary at Fuller Lodge in the station wagon which served the mesa as an ambulance. He had lost two lower teeth and would lose one more but his jaw was not broken. Two stitches were taken in his lip, but as soon as this was done and he had rested he asked Dr. Nachtigall to take him to his office.

There he meant to write down an idea which had come to him in the night.

Nachtigall and Sandeman worked on the blackboard through the afternoon and late into the evening. Several times, Sandeman jumped from his chair and began writing automatically on the board, but each time he had to stop and concede that this wasn't the miracle which had appeared to him in his cell. Dr. Nachtigall pleaded with him to go to his room and rest, but Sandeman only moaned and held his head.

When at last he could be persuaded to leave his office for his bed, Sandeman took along a block of writing paper and several sharp pencils. After Nachtigall left him alone in his room, he took off all his clothes and sat with his head in his hands against the wall, trying to rediscover the beginning of the path to his starry, starry wilderness.

chapter thirteen

"WHO IS THAT FATTISH GUY who has the office next to yours?" Maryann asked.

"I don't know who you mean," my father said.

"I saw him when I was up there collecting you the other day," Maryann said. She was dusting. It was a Saturday afternoon at Los Alamos and Maryann and my father were waiting for me to come home from playing with my friends.

"I can't think who you're talking about. Frank Woods?"

"I don't know what his name is. That's what I'm asking you. He's a really fat guy with a little moustache and goatee and he talks in a high squeaky voice. He said hello to me."

"That's Frank Woods," my father said.

"Who's he?"

"Who's anybody?" my father said. "I mean, he's just a guy. He's a metallurgist from the University of Chicago."

"Is he married?"

"Yes, he's married."

"Well, that surprises me."

"I don't see why it should. Why can't Frank Woods be married if he wants to be?"

"I just think it's funny. Putting it all together, I mean. He's fat, he talks with a high, squeaky voice, and he seems sort of effeminate. There doesn't seem to be much that marriage could hold out for him."

"I don't understand," my father said. "You think Frank Woods is a eunuch?"

Maryann went on with her dusting. She had apparently forgotten the conversation.

"Is that what you think?" my father said.

"I only said I thought he acted funny. You never talk about him, and I wondered who he was."

"Well, you can forget your suspicions," my father said. "Frank Woods is an excellent scientist and a good man, and he's happily married and I imagine his wife knows she's a fortunate woman."

"Don't get cross about it," Maryann said, folding her dust-cloth. "You never talk about any of the people you work with at the lab, and you never tell me about your work." She whisked at my father's desk, picking up one corner of his briefcase to dust underneath. "I can't help being curious."

"I don't tell you about my work because I'm not allowed to tell you about my work," my father said.

"I know that," Maryann said. "I probably wouldn't understand what you were saying if you did tell me. That's not the point."

"Well, for Christ's sake I wish you'd tell me what *is* the point," my father said. "Ever since we left Oak Ridge your nose has been out of joint. I'd like to know why. I really would."

"You haven't the faintest idea, have you Harold? You can't

imagine what's bothering me." Maryann stopped dusting the desk and stood her ground as if someone had been goading her with a long stick and she had finally taken as much of it as she could stand. "You think I'm as happy as a little bird, trudging off to my office job every morning with all those haughty women to work with every day, and you coming home at ten every evening with stars in your eyes, giving me little winks about all the grand secrets you and your friends have together? I don't like winks, you know. Did you know that? I haven't any use for winks at all. If you're out in the lab having such a great spiritual life and all, that's just fine, but I'm not in it, and I'd prefer you didn't tease me about it every time you get the chance."

"I don't understand how you feel teased," my father said.

"I feel teased when you don't come home until late at night," Maryann said. "I feel teased when you're too *absorbed* to pay attention to me. I don't want anything more than any woman wants. You think I'm a big nag, but if you'd take the trouble to find out about women, you'd see that I'm not nagging you, I'm only asking for what I need. I feel like frolicking and you give me little winks. I don't want little winks."

"I still don't understand what you mean about this winking. I don't wink at you."

"Oh, you dope, you dope," Maryann said. "You poor dope. I didn't come out here halfway across the country with you just to be around here to take care of Timmy and overhear little snatches of your high spirits in telephone conversations. It doesn't delight me to bring your groceries home from the commissary once a week and all those little wifely things. I didn't come to live with you for no other reason than to see you get ahead in your field and provide a mother figure for your little boy and see that all your meals were cooked on time whenever you chose to show up around here. I didn't come here to have you be rude to me. You're rude to me, you know, and I'm sorry but I don't love you enough to take it."

Maryann sat down in one of the kitchen chairs and began to weep. My father got up from the floor, crossed the room, and put a hand on her back.

"What did you expect here, Maryann?" he asked. "What did you think it was going to be like?"

"I expected you to look at me once in a while," she said. "I expected you to take me around. I expected you not to take me for granted. We're not married, you know."

"I know we're not."

"Then why do you treat me like we were? Why do you leave Timmy with me all the time? I'm not his mother."

"He knows you're not his mother. But he loves you. He always tells me how much he likes to be with you."

"You shouldn't leave him with me so much. I'm not his mother and I'm not responsible for him."

"He knows that."

"I wonder if he does. You've gone to all this trouble to make me say that I'm not responsible for him, but even as I say it I wonder who is."

"I am," my father said.

"Yes," Maryann said, "you are. And you should believe you are, but you don't. You don't really think you're responsible for *anything*. The fact is I'm free and you're not, I'm twenty years old and you're not, I haven't any children and you have, and yet everything you do somehow implies that I have all the responsibility and you have none. It just makes me *furious*. You can stay out all evening and dream about physics while I clean the house. I *hate* it."

"I don't force you to clean the house."

My father sat down in the chair beside Maryann's at the kitchen table. Maryann wept. Knots in the rough pine floor crowded around and watched.

"We can't even talk to each other, Harold," Maryann said into the hollow of her folded arms, her head still on the table. "You just can't make out what I'm saying, can you?"

chapter fourteen

"I KEEP LOOKING AT MY WATCH," my father said, "and trying to read the date somewhere on it. Which is ridiculous," he continued, taking the watch off his arm and showing it to Richie Mundi, "because it isn't the kind you can read the date from."

"Isn't that a riot?" Dr. Mundi said. "I do that myself. Why do you suppose that happens?"

We were in the temporary wooden office buildings at Los Alamos. My father and Dr. Mundi had been writing on the blackboard in this room. Sunshine from the skylight was coming down and making dusty shafts. The dust in the air must have been chalk dust; Dr. Mundi kept erasing every other thing he wrote and clapping the eraser in the chalk tray.

"It's just as well my watch doesn't have dates on it," my father said, "because my deadlines would be there on the back of my wrist staring at me all the time."

Dr. Mundi: Blond hair, couldn't have been more than twenty-eight. Kind of short. Sarcastic. But those tobacco stains on his fingers! ("What have you got on your fingers, there, warts?" my mother asked once.)

My father and mother have spread me thick with stories about Richie Mundi since I was very young. Richie and my father were graduate students together at MIT. I have an impression that my father expected Richie to perish as a graduate student, and was enormously surprised when he didn't. Richie had this amazingly poor little fellowship. It had been given to him by the New Hampshire religious article manufacturer for whom his father had worked until his death on the job. The manufacturer kept calling Richie on the telephone and asking him if the amount of the fellowship was adequate, and Richie would always assure him that it was. The fellowship was so small it didn't come close to meeting Richie's expenses. Richie owed money to everyone. He took a series of humiliating part-time jobs, not the least humiliating of which was constructing ornamental bookends out of brass steam fittings in a basement below a laundry and dry cleaning establishment. The gimmick was that these brass fittings were supposed to have come from the wrecks of sunken ships, and the names of these ships were printed on brass plates mounted on the bookends. Actually, the brass came from the laundry and dry cleaning establishment.

Richie had found his wife in no less likely a way than he had found his graduate degree. There had come a spring vacation during which Richie had purchased four bottles of bourbon on which he proposed to live while making a hitchhiking trip from Boston to New Orleans and back again. As a concession to his body (and possibly also to his mother, who had discovered his plans for the trip), Richie packed a quantity of cheese and soda crackers in the pockets not required for bourbon bottles. He said goodbye to my father and mother, who at that time were just married, and stood outside their apartment on Commonwealth Avenue in a surprise March snowstorm through an entire morning. While waiting for his first ride, he consumed a quarter of a bottle of bourbon and half a baby Gouda cheese. My mother watched him from the apartment window as he made a little circular patted-down place in the snow. She suggested in the early afternoon that my father give him a ride out to Route 20 where he would be likely to have better luck. When this was proposed to the frosty but still cheerful street-corner Richie, he declined the offer, for no particularly good reason. At about four o'clock, when darkness threatened, Richie was asked if he wanted to come inside for the night and get an early start the next day, and he accepted. My father heated up some bath water for him by grounding the tub and dipping in the end of the power line that didn't have the meter on it. This was the standard method of heating bath water among science students desperate enough to try to cheat the electric company. Richie and my parents stayed up late into the night finishing off the first bottle of bourbon. The next morning Richie tried Massachusetts Avenue instead of Commonwealth, and was offered several rides, but none of these promised to take him any great distance. He told my parents the very same evening that he had turned down two rides to Dorchester with bread truck drivers and one ride to Porter Square with a Harvard student. He said that he had almost gotten a ride to Weymouth with an elderly lady, but this offer had come at the end of the day when he was drunk and the lady had retracted it at the last moment in a rude way. Richie spent another night on my parents' floor, another day on Massachusetts Avenue, and another night on my parents' floor before he finally got a ride directly to New Orleans with the lovely blond girl whom he later married. She played a trumpet in a band. I think I could still find the postcard Richie wrote his wedding announcement on; my parents keep it in an old box of letters. It has a picture of the Mardi Gras on the front.

Dr. Mundi and his wife Gloria were old-timers at Los Alamos by the time we arrived. Their cabin, which was not far from ours, was the central rendezvous for all of the Mesa's card and dice activity, as well as a place where music was often played. They gave the impression of being dedicated to establishing a café society as kind of an accessory to their home. My father had invited Richie and Gloria to our cabin for drinks this afternoon.

"Shall I ask Selina to come?" Richie said.

"By all means," my father answered. "Although you probably won't talk her into it. She says she doesn't like beer."

"We'll see about that," Richie said, ducking out of the room. Selina Meisner was the lady scientist who had worked with Orr in Copenhagen. She was pretty, slim, shy, and had blond hair. When Richie towed her in from her office up the hall, she was wearing a charming yellow suit. Her usual smudge of white chalk dust was on her chin, and chalk dust was on her forehead and in her hair where she had been pushing her bangs out of her eyes.

"I told her we were going to get some space charge," Richie said.

"What's space charge?" Selina asked.

My father helped Selina on with her coat. "Don't you want to call Gloria and get her to meet us at my house?"

"That broad?" Richie said. "She has so little to recommend her." I often think that Richie and Gloria felt each other's presence so acutely that they could tease each other whether or not they occupied the same room. "But I'll do it anyway," Richie said, and he called his wife on the field telephone in my father's office.

"What's space charge?" Selina asked again.

"You'll like it, honey," Richie said from the telephone.

Selina noticed her hands had chalk on them and rubbed them together. While Richie waited for his wife to answer the telephone, Selina pretended to read a periodic chart of the elements my father had hanging on the wall.

"Get ready," Richie said to his wife over the telephone. "Get ready, because I'm going to tickle you. I'm going to tickle you right over this telephone. I'm going to give you the worst tickling you ever had. I'm going to start on your ribs, and I'm going to tickle you everywhere. I'm going to tickle every square inch of your body. And you're going to be weak, and you won't be able to stop me, and I'll never stop, not even if you scream at me and try to bite me. Now, are you ready? Because I'm going to start."

Dr. Mundi held the receiver and waited a few moments until the desired effect had been fully established. Then he passed the receiver from my father to Selina to me. We heard this boisterous female laughing. It sounded utterly uncontrolled. Gloria gasped and laughed on and on over the telephone. The very fact of her laughing made me laugh, it was all that funny. Her husband made a little smooching sound on the back of his hand and hung up.

"That sweet broad is the most ticklish person I ever saw," Richie told my father. "I'll let you tickle her some time. All she has to do is think about being tickled and she's off."

We walked out of the temporary office building onto Trinity Avenue. Soldiers in jeeps and trucks were everywhere. Trinity Avenue had become a thoroughfare for cement mixers, cable layers, backhoes, and pieces of enormous laboratory equipment. The Harvard cyclotron had been hastily disassembled and shipped to Santa Fe, and now resided in a temporary wooden lab building along with two Van de Graaff generators from Wisconsin and a linear accelerator from Illinois. Mixed in with the military vehicles were the FBI-bought used cars which picked up and returned personnel who were forced to stay at nearby guesthouses and ranches while accommodations were being built for them on the mesa. The vehicles roared on the avenue, raising clouds of desert dust through which we saw the sun low on the horizon, a darkened tomato. Incongruously, a telephone booth was now perched outside of the Fuller Lodge. It was our night to call home to Boston, so my father and I dispatched our friends to the wicker chairs on the porch of the Fuller Lodge and entered the telephone booth together. It took quite a while for us to get through to Boston.

"Hello?" my mother said at last from the other end.

"Hello!" I said back to her. It was a ploy of my father's to have me speak first.

"Timmy!" she said. "How are you? Did you get the fudge I sent? Was it melted?" I told her the fudge was fine. It had arrived not melted, but diced. The security officers had opened the package and chopped my mother's fudge up very fine indeed. I had been forced to eat it with a spoon.

My father spoke with her for a while, but they couldn't have been having too successful a conversation because my mother asked to be given back to me before long.

"Are you two still having so much to do with that girl from Tennessee?" my mother asked. "What's her name?"

"Maryann," I told her.

"Yes, Maryann," my mother said. "Is she still in the picture?"

I told her she was.

"Do you like her?"

I said I did. My mother made a fretful noise over the telephone.

"You may be disappointed, Timmy," my mother said. "Just because Maryann is with you now may not mean she'll be with you forever. Your father is going through a period when he doesn't really know what he wants. He may change his mind again soon. And when that happens, even though you may love Maryann, she'll be gone, because he's the reason she stays with you."

The telephone clicked and buzzed. The security people were listening in; someone was playing a radio in their office.

A bulldozer went by outside and I couldn't hear what my mother was saying anymore. Without saying goodbye to her I handed the receiver to my father and went outside the booth. The sun still looked as if it were trying to drown itself in dust. Selina and Richie were sipping sherry on the Fuller porch, Richie obviously having made this concession to start slowly on Selina's account. Richie was making dusty rings on the porch railing with his sherry glass, but Selina preferred to hold hers aloof from any resting place. Selina, as always, was wearing no lipstick or makeup, but her clothes and shoes were distinctly feminine.

"Tim," Dr. Mundi called to me, "will you join us?"

I climbed the steps of the Fuller porch and sat in the chair they indicated was for me. Selina went inside to get me a ginger ale at the bar. She came out a moment later, empty-handed.

"They have Dr Pepper," she said. "Do you want Dr Pepper?"

"No, thank you," I said. We waited until my father came out of the telephone booth.

"Finished?" Richie called from the porch. My father looked a little numb, but he smiled.

"I'd like to be," he said. It was kind of inappropriate. Most of my father's friends knew he had some kind of trouble at home, and of course the fact of Maryann's living with us was in plain view, but no one wanted to participate in these difficulties if it could be avoided, not even in fun. Selina and Richie finished their sherry and the conversation drifted to shoptalk on the way to our cabin.

Richie's wife Gloria had, on her husband's suggestion, picked up Nelse Nachtigall at the bachelor dormitories, and now these two awaited us at our cabin. Maryann hadn't yet returned from her job in the clerical section, so my father let us all in and mixed our drinks. Most everyone had whiskey except Selina, who went through every round with her same old sherry. After several hours, Gloria said she would like to make us all sandwiches, and so she and Selina prepared to go out and buy bread and olives at the commissary. Her husband suggested that she bring her trumpet back when she came, and this was agreed upon. Before Gloria and Selina could leave, Maryann came in.

"What a surprise," Maryann said, somewhat dourly. "I never expected to come home and find a party already made for me." She knew everyone except Selina, who was introduced to her.

"How nice to meet you," she said to Selina. "I always hear about you from the men, but I never guessed you'd be this pretty." Selina appeared not to be embarrassed by this remark.

"So, then: bread, olives, and trumpet," Richie said to his wife. "Try not to get it all balled up. Kiss a duck. Show me

110

you can do *something* right." Gloria bent over, blew on his hair and kissed the top of his head. The two girls left.

"What the hell was that?" Nelse asked Richie when they were gone.

"Don't you know how to kiss a duck?" Richie said. He brought a fist up to his mouth, blew a short puff on it, and then kissed it. "When you kiss a duck," he said, "you have to blow the feathers away and then you kiss it quick." He kissed a duck on his fist a couple of times more to demonstrate.

Maryann appeared to be in a vile mood. She asked a lot of questions about Selina and made all of us feel uncomfortable. She drank one whiskey and then another, and her questions about Selina got more personal.

"Who does she sleep with?" Maryann asked Nelse.

"I don't know," Nelse said. "All I'm sure of is that she doesn't sleep with me." This was very poor. Selina didn't sleep with anybody, as far as I've been able to determine.

"She's a cockteaser," Nelse said, "but she's an innocent cockteaser. She's serious about science. She knows it well, and she's good at it. She loves it and feels it the way we do. But she doesn't know what to do about this fact that we all have penises and she doesn't. She lets us read things while she's holding them in her lap. She doesn't keep her legs crossed enough. She bumps into people too much. She does all this stuff unconsciously, but she still brings it right up anyway."

"I had a girl friend who wanted to be a scientist," Maryann said. "She went through four years of college and five years of graduate school and got a Ph.D. But then she went to work on a government project on an island where there were only men. I guess she began giving away a few feels and pretty soon she was laying for the whole group. She literally fucked away her professional relationship; and then that was the end of her. She had to quit."

My father looked ill. He stared into his glass.

chapter fifteen

WHEN MAL THE MP WAS JAILED on suspicion of fornication with an Indian girl, he sent a note to Maryann asking her to visit him. He did this mainly because he was sure he would be transferred soon to some Pacific war zone and he wanted to speak to her before he left. This happened not many months after he had broken Sandeman's teeth with his rifle butt.

"I didn't think you'd come," he said when Maryann appeared outside his cell. It was the same one Sandeman had occupied on the night of his celestial flight. "I thought you'd say you had a headache or something. I never thought you'd come because your friend with the kid there might find out and it'd go bad for you. Thanks for the Hershey bar."

Mal was short and thin and had a receding chin. His cell was dark enough to cause Maryann to have to squint in at him through the bars. She had brought him a chocolate bar.

"Surprised to see me here?" Mal asked. "Not in the brig, I mean, in the Army. At first I didn't want to go in and then I did. I had a job in the mines in Plainsville and then I was

113

picking oranges down in Frostproof, down in Florida. Picking, I was taking home seventy, eighty, ninety a week. I moved my draft board down to Florida and then I moved it back to Tennessee. In Tennessee, the second time I came back, when I was living at my mother's house again, they called me in. But then I wanted to go anyway, I would have volunteered if they didn't call me. I like this police work. The jacket is tailored and everything, I mean it comes in around your waist. The jacket fits me like a glove. Did you see it? I think I was wearing it the night that civilian pulled the knife on me. I was wearing it then. It really fits me nice. My brother was a jerk. Iggy. He went in the Marines. The good old USMC. Know what USMC means?"

Maryann said she did.

"No, not that. I don't mean U. S. Marine Corps. It means something else. Know what else it means?"

"I suppose so," Maryann said.

Mal grinned. "What?"

"Oh, I can use my imagination," Maryann said. "You don't have to pry a couple of blue words out of me. That isn't my idea of fun."

"Come on," Mal coaxed. "You don't know. I don't believe you know. Take a guess." He peeled his chocolate bar.

"I'd just as soon skip it," Maryann said.

"Come on," Mal said. "I'll give you a hint. It's You Blank My Blank."

"That's a scream," Maryann said.

"Get it?" Mal said. "That's where Iggy is, in with all those jerks. He's in the Pacific now. That's where I figure I'll be going after this. They don't like me around here any more. That's all right. I'll be glad to get out of this dirty place. Big hot pigs-heap, is what I call it. I don't know which is worse, the Indian girls or the civilians' wives. Every fucking time you look at them, they've got their skirts up over their heads. Whoopie, look at us."

"Is that a fact?" Maryann said.

"That is what you call a fact," Mal told her. "What do you think I'm doing in here now? Because old Linda said I had her in my room. She said I dragged her in my room, which wasn't quite the way it was. You know old Linda? She's supposed to live on the reservation, but I don't think she's been there since she was sixteen. Walk by old Linda with a brown paper bag and watch her pull her dress up. Her friends tell her that as long as she's doing it, she ought to get some money out of it. She asks them how much money they think is fair. Fifty cents? A quarter? Everybody gives her a couple of pulls on the jug and calls it even. Nobody takes her home, but I took her home. I brought her back here. I just wanted to talk to her for a little while. She has it really hard."

"That's why you had her in your room?" Maryann asked. "You were talking to her?"

"Hell, no," Mal said. "I was fucking her."

This made Maryann silent for a moment.

"Why? What's the matter with that?"

"You know," said Maryann, "that there's nothing the matter with that."

At the regional high school Maryann and Mal had attended, barn dancing had been the only important form of social communication. Even though Maryann was a year younger than Mal, she had been involved in the barn dancing circuit before he joined, and so it was she who first noticed him rather than the other way around. Not that she had been attracted by him. Mal attracted few people in his high school days and fewer after that. His physical gracelessness cost him the attention of his peers, but preserved a kind of affectionate concern for him among adults, who wanted to believe he was an ugly duckling. As an adolescent, Mal managed to make this more complicated for them by being not only an ugly but a destructive and thieving duckling. He stole cars and stripped them in the mountain forests, using the parts later on vehicles of his own creation. As a young man he always owned several cars and trucks, but the police could never positively identify any of the parts as belonging to stolen vehicles. In the spring of his last year in high school Mal owned, among other things, a truck with a winch on it.

Maryann's affections at that time were all with a fellow named Ralph who played sports well and delivered eggs for his father in the family sedan before school. And so it's not hard to understand how Maryann and her younger sister were riding in Ralph's car on a Friday night in April on their way home from a barn dance in a neighboring town.

Maryann and Ralph were in the front seat, with Maryann's sister in the rear. As all the windows were rolled down, Ralph's cigarette ash, fanned to a bright red color, sprayed invisible debris throughout the car and onto the road outside. They roared through valleys cupping cold air which occasionally supported low fog, then up clay hills into warmer regions. The egg-car was powerful and Ralph drove it fast and, he thought, well. Maryann let his hand rest on her knee and his elbow press against her breast. Ralph became lost once, and when he regained the proper road, perhaps in an effort to make up time, he drove the car as fast as it would go.

Mal had recognized Ralph's car, although it passed his parents' house, where he was sitting on the front porch, at a numb speed. When he heard the long skid and the distant thump, he descended the porch steps and began walking, then running in the direction of the accident. His recollections on this subject may have been his real reason for summoning Maryann to his cell.

"There I was running down the road, not knowing what I'm going to find, and it's dark, I mean really fucking dark, you get my meaning? And I don't know what I'm going to find. I'm really scared I'm going to come on you people all trashed out and broken — arms, heads rolling around. Once I figure I might have stepped on somebody's head in the dark. Nope, nothing. I still haven't found anything when I come to the bridge, so I cross it and go up the road a little ways underneath the trees, but I still don't see you people, so I figure you just hit something and kept going, O.K.? So I turn around and walk back over the bridge, and there's fog and all this shit hanging over the water. Then I see that some of the fog is kind of lighter than all the rest of the fog, and I go, 'What the fuck?' So I lean over the bridge, and here are these yellow lights coming up out of the water. Headlights. See what I'm thinking? They're headlights. Then I knew you people were in the water and your headlights were shining out at me.

"All the time I was winching you out of there, my brother and I was winching you out of there with my truck, I just knew you people were going to be dead, dead, dead. But you weren't. You and Ralph were alive. I fucking never expected that.

"Your little sister got croaked. That was a shame. She was a pretty girl. That shouldn't have happened. But I didn't kill her, and you didn't kill her. You treated me dirty after the accident, as if I had done something to you. I fucking save your life and you look right through me, you haven't got the shit-eating time of day for me. Ever since the accident. But I was hoping you might change your mind, now that we're both here, and when I get out of the brig I was hoping you might drop in on me some time."

"I might," Maryann told him. "Let's wait and see."

At the same time Maryann and Mal were talking, another meeting was going on in Sandeman's office in the Tech Area. Sandeman, Ferrini, Nachtigall and Mundi had by this time been together for five hours thinking out loud to each other about bomb physics. Nachtigall had been at the blackboard nearly all this time, defending a radical new idea he had for detonating a fission bomb.

He explained that the idea had come to him while he was in the midst of quite different thoughts, these about astronomy and the evolution of suns. He happened to be dreaming, he said, about Bethe and Weizsäcker's solar reaction postulate, about our sun's inevitably increasing luminosity and steadily collapsing radius, about its eternal future in thermal death as a white dwarf. In death, the sun will reach an inestimable state of compaction, its atoms being pressed so tightly together that they no longer form a solid in the conventional sense because the atomic structure of the atoms themselves is crushed.

Nachtigall's suggestion was that the bomb be planned as a porous sphere of fissionable materials of a sub-critical mass which would be forced to crush inwards upon itself by the detonation of conventional explosives distributed over its surface. The fissionable materials would reach a critical mass because of their increased compaction, not by virtue of any additional material. It was an elegant idea, and the hallmarks of its elegance were all those good things — simplicity, generality, and dramatic imitation of something which is only subtle in nature — which make old scientists and technologists smile.

"Mother Dog," Dr. Mundi said. "That's it."

When Nachtigall turned away from the blackboard, he found his friends silent. Dr. Mundi was perched on a low filing cabinet, sitting on his hands. Sandeman sat in a chair smoking, and Ferrini leaned on a windowsill, picking his ear with a paper clip. Nachtigall himself sat down after a moment, in Sandeman's office chair.

"This is a beautiful thing you've done for us," Sandeman said. "There's no mistake that this is the right way to build the bomb, and my own feeling is that this is the way they will eventually be made. I see practical problems, such as how do you get all the peripheral explosives to go off at the same time, but these will be solved.

"There is every reason for us all now to be happy. We still have development work to do, but we should be happy doing that work because in developing Nelse's idea we shall be developing something marvelous. I can tell you that I am happy, and one of the few reasons I am not happier is that I — I see Emilio nodding his head over there — is that I almost thought of this myself, that is, I feel I was close to it. Never mind, it's a joy to see Nelse win like this, he's made a real triumph."

Ferrini put down his paper clip and sat with the others. "I suppose we'll really have one now," he said.

"I suppose we really shall," Sandeman said.

chapter sixteen

IN SEPTEMBER OF 1943, I went to school in Los Alamos for
the first time. There was some discussion between my parents
as to whether I would return to Boston when the school term
started but, in the end, a security policy settled the matter. It
was the never quite completely defined once-in-stay-in rule,
under which the scientists' families, after they had once come
to Los Alamos, were encouraged to stay. Family members
were permitted to make occasional discreet visits to Santa Fe
or Albuquerque, but otherwise were restricted to the mesa.

It rained a great deal in September. From my seat in the
classroom of the new school the Army had constructed for us,
I could see cars and trucks going by outside. When it rained,
I could see them getting wet down by cold raindrops, their
windshield wipers burlesquing men with skinny arms.

I did terribly in school. I daydreamed often at my desk
about Maryann. When it rained, I would wonder, is it dry at
the clerical section? The rain and the cars outside distracted
me.

Inside, every piece of property in the schoolroom was painted with the same stencil: USED. Every desk had USED on its side, every chair had USED on one of its legs. These stencils identified the property as belonging to the United States Engineers Detachment. I can remember many people making jokes which depended on the coincidence of this abbreviation with an English word, but none of these seem sufficiently funny to be worth recording here. Above the blackboards, long fluorescent light fixtures brazenly hummed mating calls at each other, but in vain: the males and the females remained immutably separated.

Toward the middle of the first school marking period, I received some unsolicited confidential advice from one of my women teachers. Mrs. Wulfkopf was a buxom, red-headed woman who, like most of the other teachers at the Los Alamos school, was married to one of the scientists working at the site. Mrs. Wulfkopf told me she had noticed that I had less vitality in class and in games than other children my age. Her solution was simple, elegant, and pleasingly Spartan. A brother of hers had found himself in the same unhappy condition I was now in and resolved to work his way out of it by regular exercise with a set of weights. Mrs. Wulfkopf outlined the exercises she had seen her brother doing in his room on the few occasions, she explained to me, when she had passed his open door. I must have looked puzzled as she was explaining one or two of these, because she felt an obligation to diagram them on a piece of my notebook paper. In a final whispered climax of confidence, Mrs. Wulfkopf told me that I might have the greatest success with these exercises if I practiced them in the nude before a mirror. I never tried them, and thus let Mrs. Wulfkopf down. She may have deduced that I never tried them from the fact that my vitality wasn't improving, but fortunately she never directly asked whether or not I was being faithful to her advice.

Not to get ahead of myself, I should say that by the time Mrs. Wulfkopf and I were entering each other's mutual confidence, Daisy and Eunice DiCicco had turned up in town and were going to school in the same building with me. I had known Daisy and Eunice in Oak Ridge, where their father and mine had spent approximately the same period of time. Daisy, now seventeen, and Eunice, now fifteen, had arrived one Sunday in the early fall with their father, whom I had known in Boston as Dr. DiCicco but who was now Colonel DiCicco of the United States Army.

Colonel DiCicco drove into Los Alamos with his two girls in a brand-new white pickup truck with chrome hubcaps and twin chrome high-riser exhaust stacks that climbed up on either side of the back of the cab. On the truck bed, secured by chromed chains, were two enormous motorcycles. They were both Harley Davidson 74's. One was painted black, equipped with a two-way radio and an entirely adequate complement of lights and reflectors: this one was for the use of Colonel DiCicco, as anyone could see by the Army star with his name and insignia painted on the rear fender. The other motorcycle, white even to the details of the twin saddlebags straddling the rear wheel, queenly even in the aspect of the deep ermine fur seat, was owned and ridden by Colonel DiCicco's elder daughter, Daisy.

On the Sunday the DiCiccos came in, a cold sprinkle was moistening the high mountain sandstone of the mesa. What vegetation had survived the dry summer at this altitude, mountain grass and dwarf spruce mostly, was being bent down by occasional shots of sleet which came and went at the extremes of rain showers. The trained eye, looking up at the darker blue storm cells wandering across gray desert thunderclouds, could successfully flinch a few moments before the showers of rain were actually felt or the flashes of lightning actually seen. Every one of us who came to Los Alamos from the eastern part of America or from Europe remembers the thunderstorms of the great American Southwest as being some of the best shows one could see.

Daisy and her father untied the clear plastic rain shields covering their motorcycles. They unlocked the padlocks and pulled the heavy chrome chains away. Daisy's close-fitting striped jersey luffed free at her waist when the wind encouraged it; her black hair drifted into the corners of her eyes and she shook her head to move it back.

"DiCicco's kid sure has filled out," Nelse Nachtigall said. He was standing beside me watching the unloading operation. There were six of us there: Richie and Gloria Mundi, Nelse, my father, Selina Meisner and myself. Colonel DiCicco's hand had been shaken sufficiently by this time, and he had excused himself to join his daughter, who had begun the unloading procedure by herself.

"His kids still push him around," Gloria said, "colonel or no colonel."

"That oldest one there can push me around any time she wants to," Nelse said. "Would you look at the fantastic figure on that little witch."

Daisy was up in the bed of the truck, arching her back, pulling on her motorcycle. Her father shouted something and waved his hands. She answered another something back to him, but the wind blew it away from us. Daisy pointed her

Levi'd fanny at us while her father brought the loading ramp around to the rear wheel. She diddled with her footbrake, making her taillight go on and off, while her father hooked the plank to a special bar in the tailgate of the truck.

"Let me take it off for you, Duchess," we heard him say just before Daisy started her engine. Colonel DiCicco was unfortunately right behind his daughter's twin megaphone mufflers when she started up. He clapped his hands over his ears and his mouth dropped open in a howl, but we couldn't hear him because of the enormous noise of Daisy's engine.

"I guess Duchess isn't going to let him take it off for her," Gloria shouted.

"What?" we all said.

"Nothing!" Gloria screamed at the top of her lungs. Daisy was jazzing the throttle as she backed down the ramp, checking her motion with the front brake on her right squeeze grip. She kept craning her neck first over one shoulder and then over the other to see the ramp under her ermine sit-me-down. Daisy's rear wheel touched the sod and she backed herself away from the ramp. She withdrew a black racing shirt from one of the saddlebags and zipped herself inside. She put on leather gloves from one pocket of the shirt. And then, with more pure, distilled *finesse* than I have ever seen on any bikey before or since, Daisy did a no-look drive-off that would have curled a stunt rider's hair. I am absolutely sure she had her eyes turned directly toward us, that is, about ninety degrees to her prospective line of flight, when she kicked into first, opened the throttle and popped the clutch. What most people do in this maneuver is get themselves aimed before they look at the crowd; or in a risky case one will look out of the corner of his eye as he blasts off. If Daisy did either of these things, she did them so well that they were inconspicuous: it looked perfect. She was out of sight in less than a second, and if I'm not mistaken I think she even took a little jump over the central high spot between the ruts before she headed off down the mountain road.

Colonel DiCicco moved the ramp to a position behind his own motorcycle. Gingerly he backed it down onto the ground with the help of Richie, Nelse and my father, all of whom helped restrain it and keep it on the ramp. Once it was on the ground, Colonel DiCicco climbed astride it and fiddled with the carburetor under his crotch. He kicked it once, twice, three times.

"Hog," he said. "Horse, sow." He kicked it several more times. The engine backfired once, but failed to start. "Horse," he said. "Sucker."

"Aa-aa," Gloria reminded him. "Ladies present."

Colonel DiCicco kicked his machine until he was nearly out of breath. The air reeked with the smell of gasoline, but he couldn't figure out what was wrong. At last he leaned it against his truck and came over to where we were standing, on the pretext of having a cigarette.

"Give up?" Gloria asked him.

Colonel DiCicco turned his head toward the thick woodsy slope containing the mouth of the mountain road. A Harley engine growled in the distance and then made a backing-off noise, as if it were going down a steep grade.

"I hope she's all right with that horse," he said. "It weighs about half a ton; I'd hate to have her bring it down on herself."

Light fits of wind pulled the rain towards us and away from us, so that sometimes our faces were stung with drizzle and other times not. We listened to Daisy's engine climbing and diving over unseen ridges.

"I wouldn't worry," Selina said, surprising us by speaking. "Your daughter seems to know how to ride motorcycles."

chapter seventeen

MARYANN, I KNOW NOW you were very important to my father
during the period following my infant sister's death. She died
of pneumonia at age seven months, in February 1944. Special
train transportation was found for my father and me to return
to Boston for the funeral. I remember it as a deeply sad three
days when everyone wept and we all missed meals. Freezing
rain. Mud at the cemetery. Ice on the umbrellas. Baby casket.
My mother hysterical. Very few people attended, since it was
the wish of the security people to keep my father's return to
the East secret. It was also their wish, despite my mother's
pleas, that I return with my father to Los Alamos as soon as
possible, my father taking personal responsibility to see that I
spoke to no one outside of his presence while we were in Boston. My mother was invited to come with us to Los Alamos,
provided she agreed to stay there for the duration of the war.
She refused, and made arrangements instead to have her
mother come to live with her. We returned to the Southwest
without her.

129

What followed was a tense period for you and my father. You must have understood that the events in Boston had been a serious ordeal for him. His feelings of guilt were very important. He hadn't been with my mother when the baby died, although this might have been possible. Once in Boston, he had wanted only to leave. His wish to have my mother return to Los Alamos with us had been transparently insincere, and she had rejected it. My mother had blamed the project, and my father's involvement in it, for my infant sister's premature birth and her tragically premature death.

Maryann, I was reminded of you because this is the hottest part of the summer, and the way the sky looks now, so cloudless, brings me back to the day at the beginning of the summer of 1944 when you and Gloria and I took that Albuquerque trip with Nelse Nachtigall. Can you recall that day? Perhaps this kind of talk bores you; you probably have more to do than I and therefore less time to spend in reveries of the old days. My father sometimes grows quite impatient with me on this score: he thinks I'm morbidly obsessed with our personal histories during the war years and dislikes talking with me about the subject.

You and my father were finishing a breakfast of scrambled eggs and bacon at our breakfast nook. This was early morning, before the seven o'clock whistle had blown, but already the sun was clearly up, ending the cold night the way the spring had ended the sad winter. You were folding up the brown paper bags the bacon had been draining on. My father looked surprised when you asked him if there was an Albuquerque parts run that day.

"A parts run?" he said. "I don't think there's a regular parts run, but Nelse is going to Albuquerque today. Why? Did you want to go?"

"Yes," you said, taking off your apron and brushing the hair from your forehead. "For shopping, I have to get a few things." You sat down to your plate of eggs. "And also for a change."

"Well, you couldn't just *go*, could you?" my father said, chewing.

"No?"

"You have a job you're supposed to be at."

"I have sick days left this month," you said. My father didn't answer you. He continued eating. You looked annoyed. Resting your face in your hands and letting out your breath so that the front buttons of your dress just barely touched the edge of the table, you said, "What's the matter with that?" My father finished his mouthful before he answered you.

"You may have sick days left, but today you're not sick."

"Who says I'm not sick?" you said, and left the table. As my father and I finished our breakfasts, we saw you putting on your lipstick and brushing your hair at the mirror in the far end of the room. You put on your light blue raincoat, looked outside at the promise of a hot day, and took it off again.

"Want to come to Albuquerque, Timmy?" you asked me. You were obviously just about ready to walk out the door: this invitation was quite generous considering how much in a hurry you must have been. I looked at my father. He said I might go with you, but qualified this permission in an undertone by saying that I must not be a trouble to you if I did go. This exhortation was obviously a bit of politics between my father and you, but I agreed to it anyway. While you were waiting for me to put on my shoes, you lit a cigarette, but soon stubbed it out on the side of the fireplace.

"Toot sweet, Timmy," you said, standing with one hand on

the doorknob. I had just broken one of my shoelaces, but decided to say the hell with it and fix it later. I exchanged fast goodbyes with my father and joined you outdoors.

The sun, having just that moment finished coloring the eastern horizon, was a cool red knot above the phantasmal skyline of idle bulldozers and Euclid trucks. As you and I walked toward the bachelors' dormitory, the inflated sun perched on exhaust stack after idle vehicular exhaust stack. It had been an hour or more since it had been low enough to touch the peaks of the Fra Cristobal mountains behind the construction equipment. The trucks, which were parked on a slight rise on the eastern part of the mesa, reached their shadows toward us. At this very moment their drivers were being brought up the winding mountain road in their convoy of used cars.

Dr. Ferrini rode by us on his bicycle. He was on his way to the Tech Area, a blue wool cap on his head and his lunch pail dangling from the handlebars. We didn't know him well enough to call out to him, so he rode by without receiving any greeting from us. His bicycle made a rasping, squeaking sound until he started coasting down the shallow hill on Trinity Avenue, after which we couldn't hear it any longer.

"Where are we going?" I asked you, Maryann.

"We're getting a ride with Nelson Nachtigall," you said. "To Albuquerque." Your hair kept getting in your eyes because you forgot to wear a ribbon or a comb or anything.

"My father doesn't want us to go to Albuquerque, does he?"

"I don't think he really cares," you said.

"He does care," I said. "He doesn't want us to go. Especially you. He doesn't want you to go."

"No," you said. The sun bounced and perched on the bull-

132

dozer exhausts. Some hawks were soaring on the windward slope of the mesa above our heads. In the Technical Area a diesel generator started and I could barely hear you finish your sentence: "No, no, he doesn't care." People kept starting engines everywhere, and there was a lot of noise and confusion, but I think I heard you say this, Maryann, I think I heard you say, "No, he doesn't care," and I think you were wrong.

Nelse Nachtigall was filling the gas tank of an old Chevrolet carryall from the fuel depot outside the bachelors' dormitory. He said he'd be glad to have us come with him if it was all straight with Harold. We told him it was all straight with Harold, and he said, "Swell."

Gloria was already in the back seat of the carryall; she had heard about the Albuquerque run and was hot for a shopping trip.

"Oh, are you two coming?" she said. "Terrific. I hate to go AWOL alone. That's what I'm doing, you know. I was supposed to help out in the PX this afternoon." We slid in next to her in the back seat.

"I didn't call anybody to let them know I wouldn't be there, either," Gloria said. "Do you think they'll mind? Richie said it would be all right. He said that if I wanted to go I should just do it. He indulges me like that. Really, do you think anybody's going to notice?"

"I wouldn't think so," you said, Maryann.

"It's sort of like desertion," Gloria said.

"No," you told her. "It isn't."

"Look at that lady's wash out on the line, there," Nelse said when he climbed into the driver's seat. "There must be three generations of clothing. Say, doesn't one of you want to sit with me? I feel like a chauffeur up here alone."

You got out and went in the front seat with Nelse before we started. I looked where Nelse had been pointing to a clothesline next to a foreign scientist's cabin. There was an enormous weight of clothing hanging on this line. Particularly interesting were the two children's stuffed bears hanging by their ears.

"Oh, look at those teddy bears," Gloria said. "What a ridiculous thing! Who would ever wash out a teddy bear?"

"Someone, I suppose," you said, Maryann.

"What?"

"Someone would, I suppose. They're out there, aren't they?"

"Yes," Gloria said. "But why would anyone *do* that? They'll never dry." She was having to crane her neck by now to see Los Alamos and the clothesline vanishing behind us.

"Oh, dear," she said. "I hope no one notices when I don't show up at the PX this afternoon."

Our way down was littered with nuts from round dark piñon trees. The cedar shrubs standing all around these trees must have grabbed their friends and shaken them just before we came. Occasional greasewoods were holding out bunches of gold flowers. A giant bug or two flew across the road from one patch of pollen-laden mountain flowers to another. The road was alternately reddish and soft, where it was mountain earth, and gray, where it was rock. It appeared that the grader had been over this stretch since the last time we were here, and in many places it had only scraped earth away from rock ledges in the road, leaving granite outcroppings like islands of ice in what I suppose would have to be the Red Sea. The farmer's cows were again lying on their stomachs when we passed them near the foot of the mesa. The farmer's gate, which Los Alamos people had been asked to keep closed, came up before us, and I got out and opened it as Johnny drove the carryall through. Once the mesa was behind us, we crossed the Rio Grande and drove across the seemingly endless desert road, a washboard nightmare. From there it was Route 84 into Santa Fe and Route 85 southwest across the hot badlands to Albuquerque. "Montoya," the mailboxes said by the side of the road. "Engle. Rameros. MacDonald."

We drove into Albuquerque from the north. All the windows in the carryall were wide open, and as we stopped for a traffic light I heard a group of little girls singing as they skipped rope inside a fenced yard:

> Who had the baby?
> Ma,
> Pa,
> It wasn't a girl,
> It wasn't a boy,
> It was just an ordinary baby,
> Ha,
> Ha.

Our watches said it was almost noon. Pools of brilliant reflected sunlight stood deep on the hoods and roofs of automobiles. Ranch trucks with the names of their ranches painted by obviously amateur sign painters waited outside supply shops. Elderly ladies were trying to make roses grow in their yards.

"Maryann," Gloria said as we were going by a grand old hotel near the center of town, "I want to take you there before we leave this afternoon. That's the Rushmore. There's an amazing bar on the first floor that looks out on the desert over all these adobe houses. It's really the nuts. I played there once on a tour before I was married."

The Rushmore looked to be of about the same vintage as the older Ranch School buildings at Los Alamos. Its wide front porch circled the entire building. Its three floors were capped by a fourth floor of dormer windows sticking out of a sloping, shingled roof. The Rushmore's opulent features testified to the era when Albuquerque had prospered as a resort playground for the rich. We waited at the intersection of Route 66 by a Phillips station and turned east with the green light. Nelse let us all off on a corner. We agreed to meet him at the Rushmore bar later.

Do you remember what we did for the remainder of the afternoon, Maryann? All I recall is walking around with you to stores on streets with odd names: Gold Street, Copper Street, Iron Avenue. Were there great crowds on the sidewalks? This is my recollection. Before Gloria had left the mesa that morning, she and her husband had hatched a plan for a big night on the town together: Richie was going to hitch a ride down on a government vehicle when he finished work and meet her here, so she would not need a ride back to the mesa with us. Gloria practically squealed when she told us about this. There was a Wild West show in town they were going to see together. Going to a Wild West show didn't sound like all that much of a lark to me, but then the Mundis knew what fun was and they had been here longer than we had. Route 66, which I had heard many Los Alamos people call the "main drag," shuffled its traffic back and forth in front of us. Taxicabs driven by men with extremely dark red skins slowed down and opened their rear doors for us, but we didn't take any. In the early afternoon, wattless neon signs overhanging the sidewalk cut perfectly black shadows in the white glare under our feet. You had the top two buttons of your blouse open, and while I'm sure that you did this simply because the day was so hot and the sidewalk was so bright, I wonder whether Gloria didn't feel slightly upstaged. There were enormous numbers of military people in olive drab uniforms on the street.

"Look, I guess I'll go on a few errands of my own before Rich gets here," Gloria said. "Sorry to be ducking out on the ride back. Be sure and get Nelse to buy you a drink at the Rushmore bar before you leave. Everything's lovely there; be sure and try it."

After Gloria left us, we went into a drugstore and spent ages looking at color postcards of Western sunsets with cactus and sagebrush skylines. We finally chose one that had purple and gold in it as well as the conventional red and orange. On the back, just above the writing space, fine print said:

> *The sun hath made a goodly set,*
> *boding of a fair tomorrow.*
> — WILLIAM SHAKESPEARE

And below that: *Albuquerque, New Mexico.*

You stood up to the soda fountain and wrote a message to your parents in the "message here" space. When you finished writing, you bought a stamp for the card and mailed it. It was nearly time to meet Nelse, so we walked to the Rushmore.

"Gloria isn't coming back with us?" Nelse asked. We were sitting at a dark table nearly alone in the barroom. The time must have been about three-thirty. "How do you suppose she talked Richie into coming down to pick her up?" he added after a sip.

"*He*," you said, "is under *her* thumb."

"Think so?"

"Absolutely."

"I like Gloria, though," Nelse said.

"Well, everyone does. I do, even. She's sweet."

Nelse smiled into the rim of his whiskey glass, as if it were the open mouth of some cannibal he had just outwitted by deciding at the last minute not to put his lips near the glass.

"What's funny?"

"Oh, your saying Gloria's sweet," Nelse said. "I'm just remembering something that happened quite a while ago, before you knew her."

"Tell me."

"You probably won't think it's funny."

"Yes I will. Now tell me."

"Well, this happened when Timmy's father and mother, Richie, Gloria and I were living together in an apartment on Beacon Street in Boston . . ."

"Was that the one where you ruined the elevator by sticking your umbrella into the electrical works?"

"Yes, but that's another story. How did you hear about that?"

"Harold told me. I live with him, you know."

"Yes, of course," Nelse said. He held out two fingers to the girl who was serving us. She brought two more whiskeys.

"I don't want another whiskey," you said.

Our waitress looked very confused and unhappy. Her hand holding the unwanted whiskey trembled.

"Oh," she said, "did I goof?"

"Darling," Nelse said, "You didn't goof. Couldn't goof. This is lovely."

Nelse paid her an enormous smile and she left. When we were alone again, you said, "Keep going."

"Well, Gloria came shouting out of the bathroom one day. She said that she had discovered she had crabs. You know what crabs are? They're little creatures that live in pubic hair and they're terribly hard to get rid of. You have to shave and treat yourself with this vile stuff for months."

"I know what crabs are," you said.

"So for the rest of the day Gloria was running around the house with buckets of Lysol, scrubbing the bathroom and toilet seat with every disinfectant she could find. It turned out what she had thought were crabs were cracker crumbs. She had been eating crackers on the toilet."

"I believe that," you said, Maryann. "I really believe that. I can just see Gloria sitting on the potty eating crackers and checking herself over for crabs. That's just like her."

Outside, through the windows Gloria had told us about, we could see the roofs of adobe houses terracing their way down the slope of a hill. Someone had decided that the glass in these big windows should be tinted, and so it was; a gray, steely light was all that found its way into the barroom from the yellow flash of New Mexico outdoors. The low stage where Gloria and her traveling band must have performed on tour before the war was behind us. The tables had a faint smell of beer about them; certainly enough of a smell to guarantee their authenticity as bar tables.

"What we want is some jerky with this," Nelse said, sort of to me. "Does he have any jerky back there?" We all looked around at the bartender, who didn't seem to have any. "It would be nice if somebody would slip out to the jerky store. I for one would be amazed if the food store on the corner didn't have any."

Nelse gave me a dollar, which was going to buy a lot of jerky, and I was sent on my way. For a dollar, I could have gone to a movie, which was I suppose what Nelse had in mind. But I not-so-fasted him. I walked out of the bar and came back in through a side door and sat down where I could look outside through a window. This seat also happened to be behind a post, putting me close enough to you and Nelse to hear you without your seeing me.

"So you've been friends with Harold and Mrs. Harold for quite a long time, then?"

"It's getting to be a long time now," Nelse said. "Fifteen years. And we've been closer at various times than I'd say we are now. A good deal of what's kept us together has been that Harold and I are interested in the same kind of work, although our backgrounds are different."

"Oh? Were you ever at Oak Ridge?"

"I was there before Harold ever came," Nelse said. "In fact, I saw you long before he did." Nelse's big hands fingered his whiskey glass with a rhythm, I imagine, not unlike the rhythm one might use on the teat of a cow one was milking.

"You saw me? Where did you see me?"

"I saw you outside Building Y-12 leaving work every afternoon. And I saw you in the staff cafeteria. You used to wear that blue and white checked cotton dress. I didn't know who you were, but I used to look for you every day. Perhaps Harold never told you this, but I was the one who pointed you out to him. We went through an elaborate plot to find out your name, but before we knew it, we used to call you 'Blueboobs' after your dress. Harold didn't want to have anything to do with my plan to get you together at first, but I finally talked him into it."

"Why? Why would you want to do that?"

Nelse made a face as if he were thinking. He brushed the tip of his nose with a finger.

"I'd known Harold a long time," Nelse said. "I knew he had the talent and training to perform well in the important research work we were beginning to undertake, but for some reason he wasn't. He was stiff. He couldn't see the whole job in his mind from beginning to end. He couldn't let his imagination take over and completely rule him. He couldn't be rapturous about his work, even for the space of half an hour or so, which would be all that was needed to make his already good ideas magnificent."

"So you figured he wasn't getting enough snatch and I'd be just what the doctor ordered?"

"Something like that."

"Something like that," you said mockingly, Maryann. "You decided that I'd be good for him, so you glued us together. Well, did it work? Did he start doing his job better once you arranged for him to get all of what he needed?"

"I don't think you understand this," Nelse said.

"I probably don't. I'm pretty stupid. Oh, excuse me, you know that, don't you? You're the one who picked me to come here without my even knowing it."

"What I haven't said," Nelse went on, "is that now Harold really loves you. What I had originally planned to be an expedient has gone much further than that. I had no idea Harold was bringing you out here. As a matter of fact, I had already made some other arrangements; Fred . . ."

"What? *What?* That sleepy little Fred you were with when

we arrived was going to be for *him?* Little Miss Oh-I-do-hope-you'll-excuse-me was going to be the next inspirational lay for Harold on your . . . your *relay* team?"

You put your head down on the beery table. Your hair eddied down into the cracks between the table boards. "I wish I were dead," you said. Your back heaved in sobs. The steely gray light coming in over your shoulder made you look as if you were in mourning. Your cotton blouse, which had the quality of paper flowers outside in the brilliance of the desert atmosphere, became silver foil in the barroom. What had been the light of the sun outdoors became the light of the moon indoors. We all looked cold, felt cold.

"I see you're crying," Nelse said, "but I don't see what you're crying about."

"I guess that is a little subtle," you said, your head still on the table. "You only just called me a whore."

"I did not," Nelse said, "I didn't call you anything of the kind. You took Harold on of your own free will, with absolutely no introductions or bribes from me. The mere fact that you never noticed me before we all came here is proof of that. What you're crushed about is a matter of pride: I've just told you that I was the one who seduced Harold to your side, whereas you had been giving *yourself* credit for taking him away from his wife. The truth may be that neither one of us did it; he may have taken a mistress at this time on some other advice. Whatever it was that got him started, the result is the same; he loves you now and he needs you. He's told me himself."

"Not true," you said, Maryann. "He doesn't care about me."

"You can go on like that if you want," Nelse said, dredging his pipe in the tobacco wallet he had just opened. "But it doesn't change the truth. As I see it, the guy is completely committed to you. He's depending on you."

Nelse lit his pipe, making fishlike smoke clouds in our synthetic cave. The man behind the bar, many tables away, had finished washing glasses and was hanging up his dish towel. It was a bit part, but he did it flamboyantly.

"We've had lots of good times," you said, lifting your head, "even since we've been here. Like when he heats the water for my bath on the stove. I sit in the tub and he knocks himself out for me, carrying water in pots and pans back and forth from the stove to me. He pours the water in so gently, and I lift my feet up. He scalded me once, just a little bit, on my leg, and you should have seen how grief-stricken he looked. I kiss him for heating my bath water for me. We have good times. But I never knew you fixed him up with me. And I don't believe he told you he loves me. That can't be true. It can't be true that he cares about me."

From where I was sitting some distance away, the gray glass was making everything outside look as if it were made of lead.

chapter eighteen

THE STUFFED BEARS were still hanging by their ears when we arrived back in Los Alamos at the end of our Albuquerque trip. Their glass eyes sparked at each other in our headlamp beams as if they were trying to light each other's cigarettes. At our cabin I expected Maryann to refuse to get out of the carryall. I had anticipated that whatever vengeance she was about to take out on my father and me would be in a night or two of isolation from us. My guess was that she would either sleep in her trailer, which was parked next to our cabin, or let Nelse drive her to the Fuller Lodge.

But instead, Maryann surprised me by coming into the cabin. Inside, moonlight coming through the windows was bright enough to show us our way. The blue checked table-cloth on Maryann's improvised dining table was luminous: reflected light from its surface almost amounted to a glare. Maryann let herself into my father's darkened bedroom as if nothing had happened.

Whatever embarrassment Maryann had suffered in Albuquerque seemed to have been forgotten not many days later, on a Saturday in early July, 1944, when she took Daisy DiCicco and me on a walking trip down into Pueblo Canyon. This was a hike I had made once before with my father and Dr. Ferrini. From the northwest edge of the mesa you walked for a short distance down a gentle slope, through a field with long grass in it, and then turned northeast for the steeper, rocky descent into the canyon.

Marching down through low spruce groves, Maryann and Daisy and I could see the peak of Caballo Mountain, three miles off to the northwest, and Guaje Mountain, about a mile to the north. Imagine us walking down through mountain woods, which are occasionally thick with low boughs. We are often obliged to turn our shoulders sideways and push through stiff pine branches. Daisy, whom I follow, is not terribly careful about the way she lets them go.

You must understand that Maryann is carrying, in a pocket, a roll of blue crepe paper. If I could see into her pocket, I would ask, "What are you doing with a roll of blue crepe paper?" But I notice nothing. The crepe paper is out of sight.

Where the gentle slopes with their low pine cover give way to the steep descending notch, we have a magnificent vista. The peak of Guaje Mountain takes the horizon ahead of us. Below lies the lower flatness of the North Mesa, and below this the opposite wall of Pueblo Canyon. Los Alamos is above and behind us, its civilization marked by the old green water tower. Straight down, we can see the brook which has made this canyon. When the wind is still and the trees around us are motionless, we can hear the brook.

Maryann is first, and Daisy and I follow her down the steep face of the canyon. We follow a path of dull blaze marks on the trees. Whenever we pass through a grove of aspen, the trees make handholds for us and support the illusion of descending a ladder. The aspen leaves rattle themselves together above our heads when the wind tells them to. The trunks are so slender that they shake under our grasp, making a wind noise even when there is no wind.

When we encounter difficult places we go more slowly. Once Daisy falls and slides a little way on her back, but she isn't hurt. Sometimes we rest, and look down into the deep canyon with the brook coming up closer under us.

We leave the steep part behind and come again into fir trees and a pine-needle floor. We make our way out of the sunlight into the shaded darkness, because now the sky is occasionally obscured by the branches of high, straight firs.

Not very much further on, we break out into an open place where the brook flows. Here large rocks divide the brook into several brooks. We leap among the rocks for a distance upstream. After this we walk along a dry portion of the bed. Our objective is the place where several large boulders mark the spring where the brook comes out of the ground. A giant Douglas fir overhangs this spot.

As soon as Maryann reaches these boulders, she peels off her MIT sweatshirt and spreads it on a place near the top of the rock where a shaft of sunlight is falling from the treetops. She climbs on the rock and lies on her back in this sunlight, shielding her eyes with an outstretched palm. The white roundnesses of her bra reflect the sunlight like a couple of incandescent bulbs. Her stomach is white, but her shoulders have pink sunburn on them. She unties the laces of her tennis shoes, takes them off, and places them almost absentmindedly with the uppers down upon the twin white cupcakes on her chest.

Daisy and I sit down on opposite sides of the brook, which is making enough noise to prevent our hearing each other even if we should want to speak. Maryann lies reasonably still on her rock, seeming to enjoy the feeling of her tennis shoes. Other shafts of sunlight open and close on the floor of the woods as the tree branches shift above us. I hear a woodpecker in a distant tree but never see him. Maryann puts one foot in the brook, but it is too cold and she soon withdraws it. I am very cold sitting in the shade of a large rock near the water.

Maryann must see me shivering because she says, "Come up here." I climb up on the rock beside her, but she doesn't look at me for a long while.

"Are you cold?" she asks, a hand over her eyes. I am still trying to spot the woodpecker and don't answer. Daisy is watching us from the base of the rocks.

"Are your hands cold?" Maryann asks.

"Yes," I say.

"Give them to me," Maryann whispers over the sound of the brook, and she puts my hands on her skin, just below the sneakers. I am afraid their coldness against her warmth may alarm her, but she does not seem uncomfortable. The blue crepe paper peeps out from her pants pocket. I lie down and put my head on Maryann's arm, all the time keeping my hands where she put them.

Who is there among us who cannot remember a brook like the one I've described, and a rock like the one I've described, and a day like the one I've described? Does yours have a horsefly soaring back and forth, now over the water, now

148

climbing higher into the air, invisible against the dark trees, turning himself on and off in the columns of sunlight? Does your day in summer have a DC-3 crossing the sky hidden by the trees above, from north to south, its two engines humming a middle-C high in the air? Does your day have a sleepy Maryann, in whose back pocket hides a stealthy roll of blue crepe paper, resting on an MIT sweatshirt?

Daisy rolls up her jeans and wades in the brook. I watch her out of one eye, the other being closed by Maryann's arm. The water burbles by a stick which Daisy pulls up out of the brook: it is black and slimy but has no moss growing on it. The stick turns out to be longer than she expects: it is part of a root from one of the trees nearby. Daisy lets the root go and it smacks back under the surface of the water. It is most likely this noise which causes Maryann to sit up with a start. I suddenly have my hands back to myself again, and Maryann is sitting up beside me. Her white bra with its sweet little adjustments is hovering somewhere around my ears, and the brook at my back deceives me into thinking that I am hearing the gurgling sound from Maryann's breasts.

Maryann rolls onto her front and lets her left hand part the water rushing past our rock. This new position leaves me a great deal more of the sweatshirt, which I seize for my head. With one ear pressed to the rock, the sound of the brook is abruptly halved. An ant begins a perilous crossing of the sweatshirt in front of my face. When Maryann lies back again, I am obliged to move. She twits water in my face from the ends of her fingers. I think we are to resume our old position again, but she brushes away my hands when I try to return them to her skin.

What happens next? Do I put the crepe paper near Maryann's hand? This is unclear. Does she move closer to it at all? Does she brush it accidentally? How does she make her discovery? Who is responsible? Is it I? Maryann's wet hand touches the blue crepe paper and instantly the coloring dye runs, producing in a fraction of a second one blue knuckle on an otherwise flawless hand. She looks at the hand and is delighted: the single blue spot resembles an opal held by an invisible band. It is in a spot where a ring would be impossible to wear. Maryann calls to Daisy, who approves the marvel. In a short time, both of them have blue dots on all ten fingers.

Then Maryann does a curious thing. She turns her back on Daisy and me. Sunlight coming through holes in the trees makes light spots and shadows on her back. Her shoulder straps are off. The clasp in back is free. Now the thing is loose; it falls on the rock.

Maryann is whistling. I catch my breath as she plunges her hand into the cold water. Her back still has these light and dark patches on it, but they don't stay stationary because she's moving, dipping, touching herself with her own wet hand, touching the wetness with the crepe paper. She transforms herself.

And I become involved. I resist, but the two girls help me to become involved nevertheless. I am very excited. Maryann's face is bright, vast, comprehending. I feel at ease, confident, grateful to them both, Maryann and Daisy, who help me off with my shoes and socks, who support my arms when I nearly trip over my half-removed trousers.

They lead me into a beautiful, damp, summer afternoon communion. They help, support, moisten, wrap, tie, blue, and fondle me. I attack them with weak blows. They return my aggression with embraces. Our clothes drop around us on the rocks and in the water as if they were words we were saying to each other. We whirl. The blue dye in the crepe paper runs: it attacks me. I am lifted up, my legs buzz. A kind of dying song builds up in the blue knot tied under my navel. The girls see this and release me. I shoot.

We throw the roll of blue crepe paper in the brook, afterwards. It is completely spent: none of it can be saved to be used again. In the brook, the blue keeps flowing out, coloring the water, dyeing the sticks and roots, blueing the boulders, blueing everything.

Maryann watches me blueing the boulders as she has blued me. Tiny beads of perspiration stand around the outlines of her hair and on her forehead. I should warn her that you must wipe these away or you will get pimples there. But foolishly, I am incoherent, I am weeping.

Walking back, I again am last. The girls climb ahead of me; I straggle. My will to keep up with them is overwhelmed by fear and exhaustion. They outdistance me.

Once, I see them waiting at a point far above me on the path. The sun waits above the girls' heads as they wait for me. Maryann stands half a head taller than Daisy. Her hair shines. She shields her eyes from the sun as she looks back at me. She moves to the side of the path, picks a straw and puts it in her mouth, and then the two girls are gone.

chapter nineteen

"I HOPE YOU DIDN'T THINK of me as *too* much of a villain during the war," my mother said to me in the kitchen recently. From our kitchen, a very large room with a redwood picnic table in the center, you can see the barn with its half-finished paint job through two large windows. At noon on most weekdays it is my habit to come to the kitchen covered with white paint, and more recently sunburn, to be fed by my mother.

"Did I consider you a villain?" I said, certainly in a rhetorical tone. "I suppose so. A villain in absentia, I suppose."

"Why did I have to be any kind of a villain at all?" my mother asked. The meal she was preparing, spectacularly enough, was canned soup.

"We should stop using this word, *villain*," I said. "You weren't so much a villain as you were conspicuously absent. As far as I could understand it, you simply weren't there. Sad things happened and the result of them all was that you didn't want to come to Los Alamos. I now understand this to have been, by and large, for the best, but I don't want you to make anything personal out of that; I have in mind the kind of feeling of infidelity there was in Los Alamos during the war."

"Infidelity?"

"Adventure away from routine. Routine implying domesticity," I said. It was beginning to be weak. I shouldn't have denied the personal aspect; this wasn't giving my mother enough credit.

"I think you're a little confused," my mother said. "I don't believe everyone of my generation regards the atomic bomb project as having been a debauch."

"No?" I said. "Not even the scientists?"

My mother could present herself so much more effectively if only she would not give me the impression that she doubts so much of what she says. I remember the feelings among the adults I was with during the war as exciting feelings. They were off there in the wilderness, throwing away all the rules, drinking and talking and working through the night. I was young when I watched this happen, but not too young to understand how people were acting. I really think I felt this sense of abandon, which I now can identify as necessary for a research scientist. I think it was then that I knew I wanted to *be* a scientist. My mother occasionally tries to give me the impression that she knows all this, in fact that she knows better. But she doesn't. How could she? She wasn't there.

"Well, as you keep telling me," my mother said, "I wasn't there."

"No, you weren't, so how can you tell me what happened?"

In my mother's face I sometimes read an expression of fear. She is afraid of me. I know this now. Even so, I suppose she is less afraid I will attack her than that I will blame her for my disappointments.

"Cheer up, sweetie," my mother said. Just this. Nothing more. It should have been enough. But my mother, though I am sure she would like to if it were possible, cannot bring me any assurance from her own circumstances that my life is going to turn out all right. Certain things have already happened to me which make me think that I'll never feel the inspiration, certainly never the joy that my father and his friends had in their lives of secret work together during the war.

"If you wanted to," my mother said, "you could count your blessings. You have an excellent education. You have bright prospects."

"Except that the prospects aren't there for me any more," I said. "I tried them and they didn't work out."

"You're not being candid," my mother said. "You've always wanted to be a physicist. Now you are one. You'll find another job."

"I think," I said, "I wanted to be a physicist because my father is a physicist."

"I don't believe that's the whole reason," my mother said. "Apparently this person Maryann whom you and your father lived with during the war had something to do with your choice."

"She never encouraged me toward science."

"Is that right? She lived with the scientists, she traveled with them. Are you sure you didn't want to become a scientist so that you could share Maryann with them?"

Certain constellations appeared to me in my mother's words: Maryann eating cheese at the table with the checked tablecloth in our cabin; the white clouds above us turning black and giving us thunderstorms at the same time of day all summer; following the antelope down on the desert plains by their dust clouds but never hearing them; the circle of glasses glittering in everyone's hands at the Fuller Lodge.

"But they didn't have Maryann after the war," I said. "She disappeared."

"Which is why you now don't feel like doing physics," my mother said.

"I don't feel like doing anything, Mother," I said.

"Least of all like talking to me?"

"Oh, God," I said. "It's just that I want to talk with someone who can help me. You can't help me."

"You know I want to."

"But you can't. There's so little I want to try."

"Having tried it once before?"

"I've never tried anything. My father tried it all."

"That's what I mean," she said.

While my mother paused, I tried to rejoin Maryann eating cheese in the airy climates of my memory. She loved it so, and she didn't care whether it was imported or domestic, Swiss or blue. In the months she was with us, my father and I bought Maryann lots and lots of cheese. But dreaming about past times will hardly get us to the end of this story: you want to hear, and I want to tell you, how some matters came to a rather solemn climax, and others came to no particular climax at all, but simply ended, or extended, or disappeared.

"Your girl friend called me this morning, while you were buying paint," my mother said.

"Yes?"

"She asked how you were, and all. But she wasn't really very friendly. I had the impression I was being interviewed."

"You didn't enjoy that."

"No, and I don't believe you would if our places were changed. She asked a lot of questions without seeming very interested. I think she was even trying to disguise her voice, but that part of it was transparent. At first I thought she was fishing for an invitation to visit you, but why would she be calling me for that? Haven't you invited her here?"

"No," I said. "I don't want her to come until I finish my work."

"Your painting job."

"Yes," I said.

My mother lit a cigarette. She snorted smoke slightly. This part of the conversation was definitely over. Still, she stayed in the kitchen with me for several more minutes, finishing her cigarette. I felt very bad.

"I'm thinking," she said, "that you're still very young, and you may be very unfair to yourself thinking that life has passed you by."

"Isaac Newton," I said, "was twenty-three when he conceived his Law of Universal Gravitation. Einstein published his paper on special relativity at twenty-six, and Dr. Orr had done his most important work in explaining atomic structure by age twenty-seven."

"All of this," my mother said, "puts you, at your present age, in your prime. You should be happy."

"I don't doubt that for a moment, Mother," I said.

chapter twenty

On one of the hot days of late summer 1944, I accompanied my father and others on an official exploring job in the desert. When our caravan of five military vehicles stopped in the town of Socorro, General Windkessel climbed out of his jeep and came over to ours. Socorro is nearly two hours south of Albuquerque on Route 85. We had stopped there to refuel and fill our fresh water cans for the push south to Engle, and from there into the desert. In our jeep, besides my father and myself, were Nelse Nachtigall, who was driving, and Dr. Orr.

"Ferrini wants to borrow a slide rule," General Windkessel said to us.

My father produced a small one from his shirt pocket.

"How do you work it?" Windkessel asked him. Without waiting for an answer, he pushed the slide back and forth until it popped out.

"I broke it," he said.

My father took the instrument back and restored it to

health. "It has no stop on it," my father said, "so you have to be careful not to push it too far."

"Thanks," Windkessel said. "Ferrini would have come over here and got it himself, only he was too busy. He's a busy, busy little individual."

Windkessel left us. We waited behind his vehicle until our turn to refuel came, and then we pulled ahead to the gasoline pumps. I thought I heard the sun in the sky caw, but looked again and saw it was a large bird which had only that moment flown across the sun. This was the time of my life when I was most easily alarmed by things: I had only to see something out of the corner of my eye that could be confused with danger and it became a danger. In my present life it seems utterly remarkable that I should have been afraid of things, then, which I couldn't see. The fact that the process of memory is so selective; the fact that I remember so vividly being afraid during the war years at Los Alamos but can never recall the thing I feared: this impresses me. I heard the sun caw, but it wasn't the sun at all, it was a large bird which had only been hiding in the sun and thereafter soared above the corrugated, rusted roofs of some poor houses where Spanish-Americans were hiding from the daylight brightness in Socorro, New Mexico . . . and this frightened me.

Perhaps what actually frightened me were the Indians leaning against storefronts and gasoline pumps. These were the poor Indians Fred had wanted to help. The women were all uniformly fat and nearly every one wore some heavy, dark material: the favorite color was green. The men looked as if they had been struck with a leg of frozen meat about the head and shoulders before being allowed off the reservation. We had heard that it was difficult for them to get off the reservation. You could scare them by asking them for their permission papers, which they were supposed to carry with them.

It was while our jeep was having its gasoline tank filled that the man with the draft letter spoke to us. He didn't happen to be an Indian, but the condition of his clothes, the expression on his face, and the tone of his voice convinced us that he shared a sense of humiliation at least as important as that of the Indians, even though the two humiliations may have been distinct.

"Are you Army?" he asked Dr. Orr, who was sitting in the shotgun seat beside the driver. Dr. Orr, confused by the question, answered with a shrug which the man must have taken to be an admission in the affirmative.

"I've got this letter here from your bunch," the man said, unfolding a soiled envelope and extracting a piece of paper. "It says I got to go in the service. It says I got to report in at the El Paso Army Base today, only I missed my bus."

The man tried to smile. We could almost hear his dried lips crack. He had laid his whole problem before Dr. Orr, who had now taken the letter and was studying it, carefully and slowly. Dr. Orr, his white hair covering his sunburned scalp, leaned out of the jeep where the canvas roof could no longer shade him and read the letter over and over.

"They must be taking men married with three kids now?" the man asked my father. "Must be, eh? I heard they weren't taking them with three kids. I got three kids."

My father interrupted Dr. Orr, who was still reading, and asked to see the letter. After reading the four lines or whatever was printed there, my father directed the man to General Windkessel, who, by this time, was eating an enormous candy bar under the metal awning of the service station. The man looked disappointed that we hadn't been able to dispose of his problem among ourselves.

When our caravan left the service station, the man with the draft letter was again at the bus stop where we had first seen him.

The events of the rest of the day present some contradictions to my memory. It must have been that our convoy stayed together until after we turned off Route 380 between San Antonio and Bingham into the northern end of the Jornada del Muerto, that desert wilderness cupped between the San Andres and San Mateo mountain ranges which we had come to explore. But once we were on the desert, our vehicles must have separated, because I don't remember traveling as a group after that. We drove on alone, crossing waterless stream beds, smashing occasional yucca and Joshua shrubs under our tires. A spectacular feature of this part of the desert was the giant anthills, some several feet high, which glistened like Aladdin's palaces at intervals of about fifty yards in random directions. Dr. Nachtigall stirred up a number of these with his tires until I persuaded him to stop. We headed west toward the peaks of Fra Cristobal and Caballo, but these receded from us faster than we could approach them. On a direction from the Army officer over one of our walkie-talkies, we turned south and then southeast toward the San Andres, Little Buro Peak and Skillet Nob.

And then, for a reason difficult to recall, our reconnaissance demanded that we split into two walkie-talkie teams and leave our jeep for some footwork. Nelse and Dr. Orr set off to the south, while my father and I walked to the north. We picked up earth samples and put them in cups from an Army messkit my father had brought for the purpose. My father and I were later to regret having been so vocal about our enthusiasm for walking in the desert. We had agreed to walk north all the way to a certain outcropping of high rocks where the jeep driven by Dr. Sandeman would meet us. We would then ride back to the mesa with Dr. Sandeman and his other passengers, Richie Mundi and Selina Meisner.

On our trip across the eastern floor of the Jornada del Muerto, as I walked by my father's side, he pointed out some remarkable sights. We saw a giant saguaro cactus that was taller than a man and had a knot of thick flower buds on its head. My father said that the flowers were open in the night and closed during the day. A field of miniature desert dandelions dropped pollen on our shoes as we scuffed through. Brilliant purple sand verbenas crouched around their friends, the creosote bushes, which smelled vile when we came close. We saw a sidewinder track leading into a hole under the roots of a shrub. Desert insects and desert ants appeared sparsely. Under our feet, the sand was not quite white, as it would be at a beach, but rather tawny, as if it had earth mixed with it. My father stopped once in a while and scooped up some in his messkit cups.

Just when it seemed that the horizon was completely empty except for the mountain peaks threatening us all around, we saw a jeep driving toward us from the southeast, very fast. The jeep's engine whined shrilly except when the vehicle went down into the cup of an arroyo and came back up again, or struck an ant mound at high speed. I was reminded of the loud noise of Mr. Poupolatos' airplane back in Arkansas. As the vehicle approached us, we saw that it wasn't Dr. Sandeman behind the wheel as we had expected, but George Rasputin, a chemical engineer from Oak Ridge only recently arrived in the Southwest. He pulled a great quantity of dust up behind him as he stopped in front of us.

"I haven't time to explain," he said. "Are you going to see Sandeman later?"

My father said we were.

"Give him his laundry," Rasputin said, throwing a great sack of dirty clothes at us.

"Wait," my father shouted over the noise of the racing jeep engine. "We can't take this. We still have two miles to walk yet."

"I can't keep it," Rasputin said, moving off. "Thanks!" he shouted, waving, and was gone. He took as long to disappear as he had taken to appear, a jouncing, noisy speck on the desert.

My father picked up the laundry sack and set it down again. "Brother!" he said. "Feel the weight of that." I tried to pick up the sack but couldn't even lift it.

"This is going to be miserable to carry, wouldn't you say?" my father asked me. He crouched down nearly on his knees and picked the sack up again, this time carrying it on his back, with the drawstring over one shoulder. He staggered forward. I carried the messkit with the geological samples. We made several hundred yards before my father had to put the sack down again.

"It's impossible," he said. The sun and the stunted cacti around us agreed with him. "Why the Christ did he give this thing to me? Why couldn't he have let it stay in his jeep?"

My father looked at his watch. "We're just not going to make it with this load," he said. The glare on the desert said he was right.

"Let me see your hand," he said. I gave him my hand. He looked very closely at my fingernails, then gave my hand back to me.

"What were you looking for?" I asked him.

"Blueness," he said.

"Did you see any?"

164

"No."

"Then I'm not going to faint."

He looked at me closely. "I don't *think* you're going to faint. You don't feel dizzy, do you?"

"No," I said. "And I could have told you that without showing you my fingernails."

He picked up the laundry bag and we started out again. The desert was still: the air had no wind in it and the ground had no visible movement in its bushes and flowers. We walked, but the rock that was our goal in the distance came no closer. My father's face was brilliant red. He breathed heavily.

"I'm not carrying this donkey's load a step farther," he said, and let the laundry bag drop in the sand. We walked on without it. "If Sandeman wants the nasty thing he can drive out here and get it himself."

I said nothing.

We walked on. Birds were soaring high up. Vultures? No. Hawks. The sun was very bright. I kept licking my lips.

My father and I rested under a bush.

"It looks like water out there, so flat," my father said. "Like San Francisco Bay."

"What?"

"I was thinking about the ferry dock. This was years ago when Sandeman was teaching at Berkeley. He was still unmarried then. We often worked late. He had an apartment on Shasta Road; we used to go back there and talk physics until morning. Sometimes we took a night off and had a Mexican dinner in Oakland, and in the early days this meant taking a ferry across the bay. The ferries coming back to Berkeley didn't run regularly late at night, and we often had to wait a long time, mostly in bars around the ferry dock."

My father's face was dark under the hat brim. Listening. For what?

"Is he going to be mad because we threw his laundry bag away out here?" I asked.

My father was lost in thought. About what? Sandeman at Berkeley in 1934? Sandeman's course in quantum mechanics? Almost everyone listened to it more than once. Enormously good, enormously beautiful. Everyone said so. Sandeman wrote poetry as an undergraduate at Harvard. But at Berkeley he was most eloquent.

"What did you say, Timmy?"

"I asked if he was going to be mad at us about the bag."

My father stood up. He touched a sleeve to his wet forehead.

"He's changing now," my father said. "I don't know."

My father said this of Sandeman. But I saw that he was telling me about himself.

chapter twenty-one

THE WINTER OF 1944–45 wasted us all on the mesa. An endless freezing rain kept us perpetually wet and cold. The gardens which so many people planted were washed away time and again by showers and hailstorms, and the poor plumbing facilities and general lack of things convinced many people to leave the project. Probably the most oppressive part of the climate was the overpowering presence of the Army, which eroded our morale more seriously than the rain. Army secrecy, Army austerity, Army hypocrisy in matters which concerned the physical comfort of the scientists and their families left us in a general depression by the time the rains ended and the brilliance of another New Mexico summer seemed at hand.

Selina Meisner had spent the winter months at Oak Ridge. Some people said that she had asked for an assignment there because she was unable to bear the life at Los Alamos. Before she left, she arranged to buy Maryann's car which was still in

Oak Ridge, and the plan was that she would use the car while she was in Tennessee, then drive it across the country to Los Alamos in the spring, where Maryann would have the opportunity of buying it back from her. When spring arrived on the mesa, Selina arrived with it, driving Maryann's car according to plan. But by that time there were a few unplanned accident scars marring the car's appearance, and Maryann no longer wanted it back. The girls agreed Selina would keep it. Selina described her trip across the country as very lonely and arduous. She said she planned to drive her car back to New York when our work at Los Alamos was over, but this time she would certainly take a passenger with her.

That same spring Sandeman — I learned years later — received a hysterical telegram from his former fiancée in San Francisco. He wired her that he was coming, and as soon as he could get free, he took a train west.

At the terminal in Santa Fe, Sandeman bought a day-old copy of the *New York Times*, left his wallet sitting on the news counter, and boarded the Southern Comfort for San Francisco. He didn't discover the wallet was missing until the train was through Nevada. In turning out his pockets to pay for a drink a porter had served him, he found a comb, one empty and one half-full package of cigarettes, a crumpled paycheck he had been meaning to deposit, keys, small change, a checkbook, his rail tickets, and no wallet. At first he was amused to see how quickly his new wallet-carrying habit had left him when he was momentarily distracted by his haste for the train, but then as he considered arriving in San Francisco with only eighty-five cents in his pocket, his mood became more sober. He hoped it wouldn't be necessary for him to see Ornberg. Ornberg was the director of the labs at Berkeley.

Most people considered Ornberg a silly prick and tried to avoid him.

The sun was doing its big red death scene as Sandeman's train carried him over the last western miles into San Francisco. Long, bleak streets with trolley wires made nearly invisible by golden smoke and fog moved past the window. To the people in Los Alamos, this would be the place where the sun would apparently be crashing into the earth, lighting all the wooden buildings on fire and frying all the seafood in the ocean. Sandeman saw a glimpse of the blue Pacific at the end of a nameless street.

At the railway station, he called the girl he had come to see, whose name was Addie Whitman. She gave him the address of her wooden tenement on Liberty Street, and he used more than half of the change in his pocket to get there on the public transportation. Addie greeted him with warm kisses and made him a drink before he even sat down. She was a slim, dark girl whom Sandeman had fallen in love with during his teaching years in San Francisco when both had been interested in the popular radical-left and anti-fascist groups of the late thirties. From the living-room window of Addie's tenement, the red and green highlights of all San Francisco could be seen trying to make their way through the fog.

Addie listened to Sandeman's story about the misplaced wallet with sympathy. When he finished by offering to spend the night in the bus station at Market and Fourth, she said that was perfectly ridiculous, he would stay with her. Sandeman raised the possibility of their being watched by FBI men who were likely to be following him. Addie replied not a word to this, but pulled the blinds and locked the door.

Addie prepared a meal of pan-fried chow mein and red

wine. When she brought it to the table in the living room, Sandeman could see she had been weeping.

"I'm sorry," she said. "I'm so sorry to be starting it now. I wanted to wait until we had finished dinner at least."

"Sit down," Sandeman said. He held her hand. They sat down across the table from one another.

"Well," she said, "I suppose the things I tell you now should justify that telegram I sent, and should justify your having left your secret project in the desert to be with me. There isn't any one thing or any one person responsible for it all, but just an accumulation of little things which make it impossible for me to live here any longer and keep my sanity.

"Last Tuesday morning the people who live in the apartment above mine were moving out. All day the moving van that was doing them was parked across the walk so that nobody could get out without stepping over the hedge. About ten o'clock the woman, who I hardly know, brought their dog in and wanted me to take care of him. She said he was in the way of the moving men. I didn't have him an hour before he moved his bowels on the rug. While I was cleaning that up, one of this woman's children came and wanted to see the dog. After the child went out, I heard a voice calling me to the window. I heard it so clearly the woman might have been in the room with me. Did the dog go number one or the other kind, she wanted to know. 'The other kind,' I told her, but what I wanted to say was, 'Your dog shat, shat, shat on my rug.' When she took the dog away later she didn't even thank me.

"After that I went to spend some time in the park down the hill from us here. While I was there I saw my other neighbor who lives on the far side of the house, up the stairs. The man who's living with me now is quite loud, and sometimes we

170

have loud fights. I asked this lady if we ever bothered her, and she was silent and acted embarrassed for a long time before she said, 'Well, I'm never bothered, but the family above you sometimes doesn't agree with me that the police shouldn't be called.' Imagine! She said that to my face! I didn't know what to say, so I opened my purse and took out my cigarettes. Then her little daughter, who she has by the hand, says, 'Ugh. Cigarettes are dirty.' "

Sandeman had been rattled by this unexpected admission of a cohabitor, but resolved to let the situation remain unexplained. Addie had locked and bolted the door for the night. He tried to assure her that everyone in the world had neighbors and neighbor problems. The weight of his advice for dealing with them was to leave neighbors alone. Addie said she wanted to move, but Sandeman asked her if she really expected her neighbors to be any better in the next place she lived.

"I don't want to move to get away from my neighbors," Addie said. "I want to move to get away from Malenkovich."

Malenkovich, Addie explained, was the big, black-haired Communist who had been living with her for the last year. She had taken him into her apartment as a charity, having been asked to do so by a friend of a friend. He had become her lover.

"The first month he was here was marvelous," Addie said. "He was scrupulously polite and gentle with me. He stole flowers and put them where I would find them. He painted pastoral scenes on the backs of matchbook covers and sold them on Market Street. He had a beautiful, even disposition. He often sang at mealtimes. The only thing which seemed to bother him was accidentally picking up an old newspaper. I subscribe to two newspapers and they accumulate around the house. Whenever Malenkovich would begin reading a newspaper and then discover it had the previous day's date, he would break into a panicky rage. He was terrified that there was a conspiracy to give him old news."

Sandeman interrupted here to say that this was a fear he also shared, and indeed it was common to many people.

"I am perfectly willing to let Malenkovich be idiosyncratic about newspapers during the daylight hours," Addie said, "but he is also idiosyncratic about them during the night. In case you miss the point, I am talking about sex. Malenkovich has brutal ways. Some of these were revealed to me during the hidden-flowers time of our relationship, but these were the milder ones and I considered them stimulating and fresh.

"They no longer seem so. He presses me for sex every moment he's in the house. I can't change my blouse without having my breasts sucked for half an hour. The beatings with newspapers humiliate me. He makes me fellatio him with food in my mouth. At bedtime he pulls me on like a pair of pants and he doesn't take me off until morning. He calls me his penis cozy. Even in the presence of other people, I'm called by this name. I'm his furry, fuzzy penis cozy and he needs me to keep him warm."

Addie and Sandeman finished their meal in silence. Addie had tears in her eyes, and before long the tears were making tracks down her face. "Damn this cheap mascara," she said. To Sandeman, she was still the same lovely person she had been five years before when they had been together often in this apartment. She still had the same graceful slimness, the lines of her cheeks were as striking as ever when she turned her head to look momentarily toward the window, and her sadness hurt Sandeman deeply, but he was ashamed to find himself thinking that her line, "Damn this cheap mascara," was out of a Joan Crawford movie. During the night, as she lay in his arms, Addie begged him to loan her enough money to go to New York.

In the morning, Sandeman set out to try to raise three hundred dollars. The first thing he did was pawn his watch to have enough money for carfare and eating. Although it was a very expensive watch, he was only able to raise fifteen dollars this way. From the pawnshop he walked toward the banking district, passing fish-and-chips shops and Chinese restaurants. He went into a bakery in the middle of the morning and bought fresh doughnuts. The day was bright and clear, and the fog of the previous night seemed impossibly far in the past.

On the corner of Fourth and Folsom, Sandeman met a man beating a three-legged dog with a leather belt. The dog lay on the pavement and screamed with each stroke the man gave it. Other passers-by appeared to be doing nothing about this, appeared not even to notice, but Sandeman couldn't ignore such suffering. He seized the man's hand and commanded him to leave the dog alone.

"This is my dog," the man said. "This is my dog, and he's a bad dog and I'm going to beat the praying Jesus out of him."

"No," Sandeman said. "You're not. You're going to leave him alone."

"He's my dog," the man said again. "I can do what I like with him. If he was your dog, you could say what happens to him, but he's mine, and I'm going to beat him until the blood runs out of his ears."

"I want to buy your dog," Sandeman said. "How much?"

"You don't want to buy this dog," the man said. "He's a bad dog. And he's going to be no dog at all in a little while." The man said this, but Sandeman saw by the pink of his eyes and the shabbiness of his clothes that he would sell the dog. Sandeman pulled out ten dollars.

"This is a little more expensive dog than a ten-dollar dog," the man said. "This is about a twenty-dollar dog."

"I haven't got twenty dollars," Sandeman said.

"How much do you have?"

"I have thirteen dollars and some change," Sandeman said.

"Well, that makes this a thirteen-dollar-and-some-change dog," the man said.

Sandeman's paying a sad old wino all the money in his pocket for a prostrate three-legged dog may not have been the most absurd thing in the world — there are, for example, knife fights between husbands and wives, bitter jealousies between philanthropists, and professional hatred among social workers all over such things as who is the better intentioned — but the act depressed him nonetheless. The man had walked a block down Fourth Street before the dog got to his feet.

If ever Hollywood decided to do a Tristan-and-Isolde scene between a man and a dog, the next moments between Sandeman and his new friend could serve as a model. The dog did all the tail-wagging, hand-licking things which ever might have been expected of him. Traffic rushed in the street, but the city and its sidewalks and buildings and ocean air seemed clean, prosperous, and generous. They walked together into the commercial district of town and Sandeman began to feel pleased.

Before the war, Sandeman had maintained an account at the Seaman's Trust Company, and so he went here first. His plan was to cash his Los Alamos payroll check and obtain the remainder of the three hundred dollars in a small personal loan. Unfortunately, he arrived just at the noon hour when the bank was very busy. He joined a line in front of a teller's window and the dog lay down at his feet. A man in a railroad cap standing in front of Sandeman forgot his money at the window and had to be called back for it.

"It must be nice to have money," a red-faced gentleman in another line commented. "It sure must feel good to be rich."

Sandeman presented his check and endorsed it on the back. The teller was a pretty girl with short blond hair.

"Hi, Tripod," she said, looking down. The dog wagged his tail.

"You know each other?" Sandeman asked.

"Everybody knows Tripod," the girl said. "May I see some identification?"

"I don't have any," Sandeman said. "I misplaced my wallet."

"I can't cash your check without identification," the girl said.

"The check is good," Sandeman said. "Can't you look my name up or something? I used to have an account here."

"That doesn't help," the girl said. "I'm sorry. I know Tripod, but I couldn't cash his check unless he had identification."

The situation was the same at each bank Sandeman visited that day. Everyone knew Tripod and spoke to him in a kind voice, but as soon as the check appeared they became indifferent. Sandeman spent several hours in bank managers' lobbies waiting to see about loans, but this was always a dead end. In one bank someone gave Tripod a bone, and thereafter the dog carried this with him and chewed it peacefully when waiting was necessary.

As the afternoon was coming to an end, Sandeman and the dog set off in the direction of Liberty Street, for the moment defeated. Along the way they met a stout policeman with a moustache who was a particularly good friend of Tripod's. After greeting Tripod affectionately, he spoke to Sandeman.

"So you bought Tripod, I see," he said. "He's a fantastic mutt. You never see this dog when he hasn't got his peter in. I wish I had one-tenth of his sex life. Big ones, little ones, shepherds and chows, they're all the same to him. Biff, pow, in to the hilt. He must have a Thing as big as the leg he lost."

The policeman went on to tell Sandeman about Tripod's master, Thunderbird Willie, whose sole means of support was publicly beating Tripod and offering him for sale every few days. No one felt the blows he gave his dog more painfully than Willie, the policeman said, but there was no other way and Tripod gave the impression of being happy to do this for the old man. Sandeman angrily asked why Willie was allowed to get away with this.

"Because there's nothing illegal about it," the policeman said, "and if you have any feelings, you'll see there's nothing wrong with it. I don't know who you are or what your line is, but my guess is that you're here from out of town selling shoes or beer. You go around to the taverns or the liquor stores and when you find somebody who wants to buy beer, you sell. The sun comes up and goes down and you sell your beer and count your money and go home to your bed. That's just the way things are. You sell beer and Willie sells Tripod."

Sandeman and Tripod made long shadows walking up the hills toward Liberty Street. Cable cars climbed past them burdened with people: men in summer suits and straw hats, dock and factory workers with drinking bellies and hard hats, blacks wearing colorful polo shirts, and lovely young girls in fresh dresses holding the hands of men in uniform. At the top of one hill, Sandeman saw San Francisco Bay, bright and blue and clogged with military shipping. The dog still had the bone in his mouth when they reached Addie's door.

"Well, I see you bought Tripod," Addie said. "How are you, old fellow? You ought to come around more often, I don't see you so much any more."

"You know him?" Sandeman asked.

"I know him well," Addie said. "Malenkovich bought him twice. The second time Malenkovich was on to the whole thing, of course, but Willie and Tripod were putting on such a good show he bought him anyway."

Addie asked Sandeman how much he had paid for Tripod. When he told her, she said, "Well, that's quite a lot. I wouldn't be surprised to hear that's the most Willie's ever had for him. He lets him go most of the time for five dollars."

Tripod gnawed his bone on the living-room floor while Addie prepared dinner in the kitchen. Midway through his cocktail, Sandeman decided to call Ornberg at his home in Berkeley. Ornberg sounded pleased to hear that Sandeman was in town, and they agreed to meet later at a hotel nearby where Sandeman was fictitiously staying. Addie and Sandeman ate their meal listening to Vivaldi on Addie's phonograph, and afterwards Addie took out her knitting as evidence that she didn't mind spending the evening alone.

As Sandeman walked outside in the evening light to the hotel, he passed a vacant lot where boys were playing baseball. There were two older, heavier boys pitching and catching, and one smaller boy at bat.

"You can't hit nothing," the fat pitcher was saying to the little batter.

"I can hit your pitching. That's nothing."

"Don't let him hit this one, Billy," the catcher said.

"Don't worry," said the pitcher. "He won't hit it."

Sandeman waited on the sidewalk in front of the hotel for an uncomfortably long time. At last Ornberg and his wife showed up in their Packard and opened the rear door for him. Ornberg drooped an especially flaccid handshake over the front seat and said his wife's name, which Sandeman promptly forgot. This was not because Ornberg's wife wasn't pretty: she was, in a Teutonic, Minnesotan milkmaid way. But Sandeman was preoccupied with Addie's money problems.

"Could we please change the radio to talking?" Ornberg's wife asked her husband. "You said we could have talking on the way back if I agreed to have music for you on the way here. I don't care what the program is as long as it's talking instead of music."

"All right," Ornberg said. "As soon as this song is finished."

"I don't want to wait until this song is finished," she said. "I'm bored and tired of it now. I just want to hear someone talking."

She wrenched the radio dial in and out of resonance with several stations before she found a program in which grade school students were being interviewed by an adult with a sugary voice. When the children began to sing, she found a newscast and then a cooking program to carry them through to the Ornberg home in Berkeley.

The Ornbergs lived in a low stucco house on the side of a hill. Flowering bushes surrounded their backyard, where Ornberg and his guest sat at a picnic table and drank coffee. Ornberg, whose fundamentalism began with a deep personal conviction toward his stoical Midwestern religion and ended no one knew where, suggested in a laughing voice that there was a forest fire danger and Sandeman ought to keep better track of his cigarette embers. He spoke at enormous length about the work going on at his laboratory, using the first names of people Sandeman had never met and claiming the success of his results in terms of homemade indices Sandeman felt sure could be demonstrated to be nonsense. Although Sandeman was convinced several times that he had heard Ornberg say something which amounted to taking the names of mathematical axioms and physical laws in vain, he remained silent. The lateness of the hour, the remoteness of the possibility that Ornberg would help him, and the stinging sense of humiliation at having paid thirteen dollars and some change for Tripod in front of all San Francisco dulled his wits.

"Look, I'm in the middle of a small embarrassment," he said when there was a pause. "I went away and left my wallet sitting on a newsstand in Santa Fe. I have a paycheck with me, but I couldn't find any bank today that would cash it without identification."

"That won't be any problem," Ornberg said. "I'll call my bank in the morning and tell them you're coming. You can cash it there."

Grateful to Ornberg for having promised this rescue, Sandeman let him talk from the time the moon rose until it passed overhead and behind them, out of sight. During part of the night, Sandeman walked about the small yard, touching the boughs of the flowering bushes and smelling their fragrance while his host droned on at him from his seat at the picnic table. Sandeman began by hoping to remember some of the more blatant absurdities, thinking that they could be confuted later by a simple effort with paper and pencil, but long before the moon disappeared behind the roof he was looking forward to forgetting the whole discussion. Ornberg took him back to the hotel shortly before morning and Sandeman crept in beside Addie a half hour later.

Sandeman and Addie rose at ten and Sandeman walked directly to Ornberg's bank. There they said that Ornberg had an account but he hadn't called them about vouching for any check. Sandeman called Ornberg at his office and was directed to several laboratory extensions before Ornberg could be located. When Ornberg was told that he would have to come downtown to the bank in person to vouch for the check, he said he was having a very busy day and that would be impossible. He said he had twenty-five dollars cash in his wallet and offered to send someone down with this in his car, but Sandeman said he needed three hundred. Ornberg's reaction to the size of this need was confused and indignant. He volunteered the judgment that three hundred dollars was an unreasonable amount for professional associates to keep available for one another, but repeated his offer of twenty-five if that would help. When Sandeman tried to explain that twenty-five dollars wouldn't do him any good, Ornberg excused himself from the telephone and hung up.

The last option Sandeman had available was a telegram to General Windkessel, who might be persuaded to send a money order drawn from Sandeman's petty cash account which could be replaced later. At the Western Union office he sent a short message which he paid for out of a five dollar bill Addie had given him from her sugar bowl that morning. He checked the office for a reply at one, two fifteen, and three forty-five, waiting meanwhile in an attractive park where birds sang and girls too young to be believable as mothers sat on benches and rocked carriages. When Sandeman's reply came shortly before five that afternoon, it was entirely in the ridiculous code which General Windkessel insisted every member of the Los Alamos staff use in written communication. The cipher for this code had been lost, of course, with Sandeman's wallet, so he threw the telegram in a wastebasket.

Returning to Liberty Street, Sandeman found Addie in a strange, panicky frame of mind. She listened to his account of what had happened at the bank, but something about her manner let him know that it didn't really matter why he didn't have the three hundred dollars. The only real thing was that he didn't have it. She had given Tripod the meat they might have had for dinner. A letter had come from Malenkovich saying that he knew Sandeman was staying with her. Addie was weeping.

"I don't know why I feel so sad," she said. "Princess Lena says things are never as terrible as they seem, and I know that's fundamentally true. Sometimes I feel as if my arms were tied to my waist with silken cords and a robber had forced a handkerchief into my mouth, but I really know that everything that happens to me is my own fault. I know I should send you and Tripod away and call the police and tell them everything Malenkovich has done to me and they'd put him in jail. This is what I know I should do but I can't because I feel a special love for each one of you even though you all let me down and take advantage of me."

Sandeman asked her who Princess Lena was.

"Princess Lena is on the radio every day at three thirty, on the Treasure Hour. I think she must be the most marvelous person alive. I can't believe she drives her car to work and buys groceries in shops like the rest of us, but she must, I suppose.

"Today she read a story about things falling down. Petals fall from flowers when the wind blows through them. Water falls down from fountains. Fruit falls from trees. Man falls from grace, I suppose she neglected to say. Her voice was as clear and cool as a pool. She made me feel she was telling the story just for me.

"The stories Princess Lena tells are simple but their clarity and spareness only make me see the scenes and the people more vividly. The honesty of her voice becomes part of the trees of the enchanted forests and gets lost in the music of the brooks. I feel a great pleasure in meeting new people in her stories who never say anything stupid or dull. They don't talk about twats or cocks like Malenkovich and they don't let themselves be bullied like you. And if there's a dog, you can be sure he wouldn't be a pathetic three-legged thing who takes part in a sadistic con game.

"At the end of the hour, I feel this strong weepiness coming back again, as if the final loneliness were almost here. At sign-off, Princess Lena says how she loves me just the way I am, because I'm myself, and there's no other person in the world exactly like me. Most of the time I can't even finish listening to that before Malenkovich comes in and wants to mount me before dinner."

Later that evening, as Sandeman was packing his bag and getting ready to leave, he noticed that Tripod's bone was on the middle of the living-room carpet but Tripod was gone. Addie, who had been weeping in her bedroom, came out long enough to say goodbye.

"You tried to help me," she said, embracing him. "It's not your fault you couldn't."

"You'll have the money tomorrow morning," Sandeman said. "I'll wire it from Santa Fe. Please don't cry any more. There's a good girl."

But by the time Sandeman had reached Santa Fe, Addie

had climbed into a warm bath with the kitchen knife which had been her friend in dreams for a long time and the two of them had made loans, money, and other impersonal, mercantile sophistications more or less irrelevant.

chapter twenty-two

WHEN DID WE VISIT GLORIA in the hospital?

April 21st, 1945.

Why was she there?

She was dying of cancer.

Which hospital was this?

The Albert General Hospital in Albuquerque, New Mexico.

And what is cancer?

A random growth of cells which do not fit into the order of animal systems, and which these systems can generally do without.

Who, besides myself, visited Mrs. Mundi?

Her husband, Richard Mundi, B.S., M.Sc., Ph.D., physicist, mathematician, prankster, bongo player. Selina Meisner, Dr.Phil., physicist, refugee, cockteaser. Harold MacLaurin, Ph.D., physicist, fluid mechanicist, potential scientific clairvoyant, adulterer.

How did Mrs. Mundi greet her visitors?

Cheerfully. Gratefully. Palely but smiling.

What did her guests bring her?

Flowers, including roses, cactus flowers and sunflowers. Candy, including a Hershey bar and a small carton of Turkish Toffee, the latter being from her husband.

How did she look?

Well, except for her color, which may have only appeared pale beside the sun-darkened skins of her visitors.

Was she sitting up or lying down?

Lying down in bed. But she asked her husband to crank her head up.

And he did?

Yes.

Then what happened?

She asked the answers to specific questions about people at the Los Alamos project not present in the room.

Such as?

Such as, "Was the Hungarian still playing his piano all night?"

And was that answered in the affirmative or negative?

The affirmative.

And there were other questions?

Yes, but they are scarcely worth recalling individually. More important was the overall impression one received listening to her talk.

Which was?

Which was that she expected to die before ever seeing any of these people again.

And what is dying?

Dying is apparently the remarkable event after which living, organic material is free to degenerate from a very sophisticated, highly ordered state into a less useful, more random state.

Then it is possible to make thermodynamic distinctions between living and nonliving things?

Precisely. If all phenomena observed in living organisms can be described by the regular physical laws governing the atoms which make up that organism, then the only difference between living and nonliving things would seem to be that all living organisms violate the Second Law of Thermodynamics, the law which says entropy must either increase or remain constant.

And by entropy is meant what?

Entropy here would be an index proportional to the logarithm of the probability assigned to any specific motion. The most chaotic, random type of motion in a physical system corresponds to the greatest value of the entropy index, while physical motions which show a measure of order and coherence are assigned lower values of entropy. The laws of thermodynamics include the statement that in any process taking place within an isolated system, the entropy of the system either increases or remains constant.

And this law is allegedly violated by living things?

Yes. A plant growing absorbs simple inorganic salts and water from the ground but produces marvelously complex protein molecules. In nearly every life operation, the product structure is much more ordered than the materials which are synthesized. Order increases, accompanied by a decrease in entropy.

Violating a thermodynamic law?

Only apparently. If one supposes that a plant, as it grows, gives up entropy somehow to its surroundings, then the great relative order of plants, and in turn of animals, who eat plants for food, is justified.

And how would plants give up entropy?

The solar radiation falling on earth has an entropy deficiency in addition to the energy it carries, which plants are welcome to use.

How would that come about?

Solar radiation reaches the earth in a hybrid state, having a sharp spectral distribution corresponding to the high temperature of the solar surface, but with an energy-density corresponding to the comfortable temperatures of the surface of the earth. This is an improbable state, therefore a low entropy state on the surface of the earth.

Meaning?

Meaning that as long as the sun makes available its entropy-deficient energy, living things can apparently make incredibly ordered life structures out of air and soil. And when that facility is interrupted, the life structures degenerate into evidences which are no longer so purposeful.

And when they are no longer so purposeful, are they dead?

Yes.

So Gloria presumably knew she was going to die?

Everyone knows he is going to die.

Quite right. Let us change the subject. Was there any discussion of a matter which related to the security of the project at Los Alamos?

Mrs. Mundi showed us letters which she received from her husband written at Los Alamos.

What was unusual about these letters?

They apparently had been cut up by Dr. Mundi before he had put them in the envelope, forcing anyone who wanted to read them to piece them together like a jigsaw puzzle.

And what purpose did all this serve?

The Mundis explained that this was to confuse the censors.

What happened next?

Dr. Mundi told his wife to take it easy on the cleavage.

What did he mean by this?

He meant she shouldn't let the neckline of her nightgown fall so low.

And did she take his direction and make an adjustment to her nightgown?

Yes.

It was said before that Mrs. Mundi looked pale in comparison to her visitors. Had she been hospitalized long by this time?

Two months and some days.

Not a particularly long time, then.

It seemed like a long time at Los Alamos, because such a great deal was accomplished. Nelson Nachtigall's suggestion about implosive detonation and his subsequent work on its theory and design had made the original schedule calling for a test explosion in the coming summer seem realistic. It was evident that the supplies of fissionable materials from Oak Ridge and Hanford were going to be adequate to build something like three bombs by late summer.

The work on the atomic bomb progressed while Mrs. Mundi grew paler?

Yes.

As if what Mrs. Mundi needed were an artificial sun.

Yes, if you like that interpretation.

Meanwhile, what was the real sun doing?

It was slowly getting brighter.

Why?

Because it happens that helium, the end product of the carbon-nitrogen thermonuclear reaction in the interior of the sun, is less transparent than the original hydrogen which begins the cycle. As more hydrogen is transformed into helium, the blanket of gases on the surface of the sun becomes more opaque to radiation and the resulting accumulation of energy in the central parts leads to a rise in temperature and an increasing rate of energy production. By the time the supplies of hydrogen in the sun are exhausted, solar radiation will have increased to over a hundred times its present level.

Did Mrs. Mundi seem worried about the imminent death of the sun?

No. In fact, as said before, she may have been speculating on her own death.

What leads you to this conclusion?

She played a trumpet solo for her guests. This was the concert that she had promised us from her arrival at Los Alamos, but had never gotten around to before this time. It was lovely and achingly melancholy as only an unmuted trumpet in a small room can be.

What were the colors of the trumpet?

The colors of the trumpet were the colors of the people's clothing in the room, and the color of the flowers on a table nearby. Brassy gold. Red. The blue of her husband's suit. White for the sheets. But predominately gold. Gold and round at the end like the sun.

Does it seem appropriate to compare looking into the end of Gloria's trumpet with looking at the sun?

Yes. The feeling of listening to the sounds she played really begged to be compared to the feeling one has looking at the sun. And the visual experience was there, too: the yellow, sharp, shininess of the horn, red roses reflected in the bell, buttons on her husband's coat reflected also.

She paused in the middle of her concert, did she not?
Yes.
And when Mrs. Mundi asked about Maryann, did they tell

her that she and Nelson Nachtigall were to be married the following month?

Yes.

What was her reaction to this?

She betrayed very little interest in this; one thinks because my father and I were standing right there, and it would have been awkward for her to ask a lot of questions about how it came to pass that Maryann was marrying Nelse. A common speculation was that Maryann was pregnant, of course, and Mrs. Mundi may have heard this from someone. The speculation turned out not to be true, as far as I have been able to establish.

And there was some other news?

Yes, rumors about Dr. Sandeman. It was being said that the FBI was harassing him about a sudden trip that he was reputed to have taken to San Francisco to see his former fiancée, who was supposed to have threatened suicide. The rumors said he had spent two nights with her in her apartment and she had killed herself after he had left.

Was very much further said about this, other than to repeat the rumor?

No, and Mrs. Mundi took up her trumpet again. She played, on her husband's request, the solo part from Mozart's Horn Concerto No. 3 in E-flat major. She did it extremely well. We all sat by her bed, some of us at the foot of her bed, and it was easy to imagine that some kind of party was going on. Mrs. Mundi's lips were all the redder where they met the instrument because her face was pale: blood on snow.

And as her visitors left, and were driving back to Los Alamos, Dr. Mundi was playing with a rubber band he had found on the night stand in his wife's room, isn't this right?

Yes. He was wrapping the rubber band around and around

the fingers of one hand. When it was pointed out to him where the rubber band had come from, he said, "God took Gloria away and left me with this rubber band. God is a lousy packrat."

chapter twenty-three

"I THOUGHT WHAT WENT ON in the parking lot after the reception was a little crass," Richie Mundi said.

"It did spoil things, didn't it?" my father replied.

"The Feds would like to be able to prove that more of those things weren't accidents," Richie said. He was talking about the two engineers who had smashed their cars into each other in the parking lot of the Hotel La Fonda in Santa Fe after Maryann and Nelse Nachtigall's wedding reception. The engineers were drunk and had been having a fist fight, and apparently had jumped in their cars and smashed each other until neither car could move.

This was the day after the wedding. My father and I were in Gloria and Rich's apartment, visiting Richie. He had let the place run down since his wife had entered the hospital. Boxes of trash were piled in the hallway. The telephone was on the floor in front of the sofa. Through an open door, one could see a drinking glass on the bathroom sink with two candied cherries hardening in the bottom. A paper bag on the

193

floor in front of the sofa contained two packages of cigarettes. Another bag held a loaf of bread.

"Crude bastards," Richie said. He stood up and stretched. This must have been a Sunday, because the wedding had been on a Saturday, the reception Saturday night. We had been talking about the wedding. Richie had been talking about it, actually. My father and I hadn't much to say. We had been at the wedding, and we had stayed for the reception, but we hadn't seen half of what had gone on, the way Richie told it. Richie had been the best man.

The general shabbiness of the apartment was contributed to by odors from the small kitchen. Someone hadn't been caring for his dishes and garbage.

"I wish the hell Gloria could come home," Richie said. "Then maybe I'd feel like doing something."

"Not very pleasant," my father said.

"Not very pleasant at all," Richie agreed.

The loaf of bread in the paper bag sat very still on the floor. It wasn't going to be eaten. It was going to be forgotten, and it was going to get very hard, and eventually someone would throw it away.

"Did I tell you that Maryann was over here one day before I took Gloria to the hospital?"

"No."

"I was pretty surprised. I came in and found her in her slip, wearing one of my shirts. Wouldn't that strike you as kind of funny? I mean, coming home and finding a girl you didn't know all that well visiting your wife, and she's got her dress off and she's wearing one of your shirts?"

It didn't strike either me or my father as funny. She used to wear my father's shirts the same way. I thought of her. Maryann. It seemed as if I hadn't seen her in so long.

"Why did she have her dress off?" my father asked.

Richie hadn't heard the question. He was hanging a pair of trousers on a hanger. He was running water in the bathroom. He was trying to throw the cherries out of the drinking glass down the toilet, but they wouldn't come out. He pried them out with an index finger.

"Why did she have her dress off?" my father repeated as Richie walked in front of us.

"I don't know," he said. "They were doing something to it," he said. "They were sewing on it."

Richie was putting his arms through the sleeves of a shirt. He stopped, bent down, and sniffed at a glass beaker that was filled with mercury. He dipped some of the mercury out and transferred it to a device that looked like a medicine dropper suspended above the beaker. Drops of mercury slowly grew at the bottom of this device and fell into the beaker with a hollow rhythm.

"Guess what this is," Richie said. My father and I came over and looked at it. It appeared very simple, but we didn't know what it was doing. The drops of shiny metal grew and fell regularly. We still couldn't guess.

"Gloria loves this thing," Richie said. "I really should wait and let her show it to you when she comes home."

The drops dropped. We watched. We didn't see the point of it. It was only mercury falling into a glass beaker.

"Watch this," Richie said. He disappeared into the bedroom. When he returned, he was carrying a single white rose in a brass vase. He put the vase down on a bookcase at the opposite end of the room and returned to us. He sat in a chair. "Now," he said, "we wait."

We waited. Richie's apartment wasn't looking any more organized as time went on. He had been dressing while talking to us, and now his pajamas were lying all over the place.

Less than a minute later, Richie jumped up and sniffed the beaker.

"Smell that," he said.

My father and I sniffed around the beaker. There was an overpowering odor of perfume. The intensity of the odor above the surface of the mercury was so sweet and heavy that we were scarcely able to inhale it.

"It's an odor amplifier," Richie told us.

My father smiled. He must have known then how it worked, but Richie explained it to us anyway.

"The growing drop adsorbs the faint odors of the room on its surface," Richie said, "but when it falls into the beaker, it gives up most of its surface area. Most of the odor is then released back into the air, but it stays in the beaker above the surface of the mercury because odors are heavier than air."

The odor amplifier dripped on, unaware of having been explained.

"I suppose all you would have to do is cut an onion in the kitchen . . ." my father said. He didn't finish his sentence. Time dripped by as we watched.

"Or fart a half a mile away," Richie said.

I had a different vision of how Richie's odor amplifier might be demonstrated. Might it remember things it had smelled weeks ago? If Richie had made it smell a gardenia, for example, on the previous day, would there still be left some of the gardenia smell of yesterday mixed in with the overpowering rose smell of today? Could I sniff the beaker and sort through past odors? Would they be distinct? What would I find there? The rose of today. Cooking odors, perhaps. Tobacco smoke. Gloria's nail polish. The floors might have been waxed recently: I would smell floor wax. But what of the more subtle things: would I, for example, smell the spices on Gloria's shelf behind her stove? Or the hand soap in the dish beside the tub?

The fantasy plagued me. But it wasn't any of these past smells I really cared about. It was Maryann. Her coat: would it smell of mothballs? Her dress, the one she had removed: how would it be represented? The speculation teased me until the full image of Maryann's dress lay beside me on the sofa. I had seen her clothes so often before: they were always ironed and neat, and when you found them lying out and put your face down into them, they smelled faintly of sachet.

Maryann's imagined dress became her wedding dress. It was amusing to think I had never seen it before she wore it in the wedding. I had seen every other piece of clothing she owned, but never her wedding dress. So often, in our log house, we had washed our clothes together. They dried on rope lines hung before the fireplace. The clothes dried together, and I saw all Maryann's, and she saw all mine, but the wedding dress was never there. Did she borrow it from one of the European wives? Did she buy it in Albuquerque? Had she brought it from Tennessee and kept it all the time, locked in a secret closet in the trailer, its whiteness hidden away from all light? And when it came time to put the wedding dress on, and it was laid out on a bed at the women's dormitory, who had been there to help? Most probably, Selina Meisner had been there. I knew the two misunderstood each other. Maryann was never able to appreciate Selina's role in the scientific community; each thought the other in some way brazen. But there it was: Maryann would need Selina's help before the wedding. Gloria was locked up in the hospital, and Maryann had made few other friends since coming to Los Alamos. What would the girls talk about while Maryann dressed? Selina was looking for a passenger to ride back to New York with her after the test. She had placed an advertisement on the main bulletin board at the Fuller Lodge. She was interviewing people; perhaps she told Maryann about these.

And what of the wedding itself? Our invitations said it was to be held at three o'clock in the Catholic cathedral in Santa Fe. At two-fifteen, my father and I were waiting outside the cathedral with several other guests when Richie Mundi and Nelse Nachtigall drove up. Their tuxedos were the same: you couldn't tell the best man from the groom. We waited for the priest to open the wooden doors under gray, cold skies. The overcast seemed to be thousands of miles above us, the highest one I've ever seen, but the clear air between us and the clouds allowed us to see these in enormous detail, their hammered and scarified undersurfaces making heaven look remote and yet real, as it does in a hymn.

Richie showed us the rings. The groom's ring, like the bride's, was a traditional gold band, but it was unusually thick and heavy. In retrospect, I can see that the ring was another one of those clues whereby one discovers someone else's pathetically mistaken convictions about the future: Nelse, in choosing the rings, obviously saw his marriage going on midway into the next century, and pictured himself requiring a ring with enough gold in it to withstand the erosion of something like a thousand years.

When the priest arrived, the groom's party left us to our own amusement inside the cathedral. It was far more splendid inside than I had been prepared for. Architectural embellishments whose names I shall never know grew from the walls and climbed up into the webs of the quite high ceiling. Rose windows at improbable heights above the floor cast down paths of dusky colored light which, like the tapered filaments from which the lamps hung, seemed capable of swinging. My father and I took seats in the pews at the front of the church. Some details of the altar before us were inspiring. The wooden carvings lacked nothing but gargoyles, and I won't really swear that these were absent. Screens, tapestries, and mottos made symmetrical patterns. The priest came out to speak to the father and mother of the bride, who had arrived just after us and were now sitting a few rows ahead. He knelt on one knee and genuflected to the altar as he returned behind the stages. More people arrived and took their seats. From somewhere behind the altar, as if he had come to the most eloquent part of his sermon, or to the point in a litany where one's inner imaginings are accidentally identical with the invoked response; from behind the altar, as if snatching us by surprise and hastening us the last steps into his real church, the priest turned on all the lights, bank by bank, the whole clanking, switching operation requiring the best part of a minute, until the interior of the church was bright.

I was enjoying being left to roam around in the provinces of my own thoughts. I was remembering and wondering this and that. Imagine how annoying it was when the older woman behind me complained to her friend, "It's three o'clock. Weren't they supposed to start at three?"

Later, at the La Fonda, where the reception was held, people continually clinked their champagne glasses with their knives as a signal for the bride and groom to kiss. Old Dr.

Orr, who was sitting beside us at the table, was one of the more spirited clinkers. He clinked loudly and then laughed whenever Maryann and Nelse kissed.

"Wonderful wedding," he said to my father and me. "I loved very much 'Ave Maria' at the end of the service. I am not Catholic, but the solo of 'Ave Maria' was so beautiful I weeped. It was just as if the solo was made for all of us alone, and was not 'Ave Maria' but 'Ave Maryann.' "

Neither my father nor I said anything.

"Why a Catholic wedding?" Dr. Orr asked us. "Nachtigall isn't Catholic, is he?"

"Maryann is," we told him.

We were all seated around a long dinner table. The puffins in dinner jackets who served us were rumored to be FBI men in disguise, but this rumor was never firmly established. We knew that the bartender who worked the four to eleven shift was a Fed because someone had once tricked him into defending the Washington Senators in a sports discussion, but the other serving personnel at the La Fonda were too close-mouthed to give themselves away. At the table were: the Di-Cicco family, (Daisy looking very grown-up in a purple velvet dress), Selina Meisner, Richie Mundi, Dr. Orr, Nelse Nachtigall, my father, and myself.

The waiters spilled wine on the tablecloth all through the meal. The talk around the table drifted to technical matters, and it's possible this was being done purposely to get one of the waiters to tip his hand with an anxious facial expression. Richie Mundi and Nelse Nachtigall were particularly keen on this game. They drew schematic diagrams of implosive lenses on their table napkins and outlined circuit diagrams of a fusing device they called the "initiator" on a corner of the tablecloth. When dinner was over and the party adjourned to the card-playing room, Rich and Nelse hid behind a pillar in the dining room.

"They're all Feds," they reported to us later. "They scooped up the napkins we wrote on and the tablecloth and packed them in somebody's briefcase."

After the meal, there was a receiving line. I met Maryann's parents again, but of course I was nothing to them, they didn't even remember me. The bride bent down to let herself be kissed by me, but unfortunately I kissed her just as she was using her handkerchief, and she barely saw it was me. This may have been because she was distracted by the person standing just behind me, my father. When his turn came, they spoke to each other, but this was lost to me. What I remember instead is the jarring feeling of seeing Maryann extend her hand to be shaken. My father took her hand, but covered it with his other hand, and he didn't shake it, he held it a moment, then kissed it and passed on.

Later on, during the dancing, Maryann sat on the knee of a person she called Uncle Pete. He was fat and had a red face. While Maryann was dancing with another relative, Uncle Pete came over to talk to my father and me. I'm sure he hadn't a clue about what our relationship to Maryann had ever been; he just considered us available ears.

"Doesn't she make a beautiful bride?" he asked us. "She's my sister's girl. My sister had two girls, but one of them, Maryann's younger sister, drowned. That was a damned shame. She was a little blond girl, absolutely lovely. She was devoted to Maryann, followed her around and all. I've never seen a more lovely young woman in a casket. It's hard to forget her. I almost called Maryann by her sister's name when she was sitting on my lap a while ago."

Uncle Pete went off to freshen his drink. Before he was

201

gone very long, Maryann's father came over to us. He acted as if he had never seen us before and introduced himself to us as "the father of the bride."

"I've just come from the kitchen," he said. "A waiter came up to me and asked me if I'd like to meet the chef. I went with him back in the kitchen and shook hands with the guy. 'How did you enjoy the meal?' he asks me. 'Just fine,' I says. Then he just stands there looking at me for about five goddamn minutes. I'll be damned if I'm going to tip the bastard. The cost of this thing is sky-high already without giving the chef ten dollars or something ridiculous like that."

Maryann's mother hovered around while we were talking to her husband. She never came over to speak to us, and in a way we were unfortunate not to have the benefit of her thoughts, when one remembers that the only other time she had spoken to us, Mrs. Moriarty had all but warned us this day was coming. She had said she was glad to see Maryann get ahead. We should have guessed that Maryann would tire of us and pick someone else.

Dr. Sandeman arrived at the reception late. He appeared overworked, nervous, tired. His clothes led us to believe that he had spent the day on the desert, presumably at the test site where my father and I had misplaced the laundry bag. He wore jeans and a work shirt, a wide belt, and his ever-present porkpie hat. The hat accompanied him everywhere, whether he was in ranch clothes in New Mexico or in a business suit in San Francisco. The hat was such an important symbol of Sandeman and the Los Alamos days in physics that the first issue of the Journal of the American Institute of Physics, which began publication after the war, included as a cover piece a photograph of the Berkeley cyclotron with Sandeman's porkpie tossed on it.

On this evening, the presence of a dusty, overworked Sandeman in the room changed everyone. The band played on, and the dancing continued, but people said less to each other. Sandeman sat and drank by himself for a while before he spoke to my father.

"Why doesn't anybody want to do his job?" he asked. "Is that too much to expect of anyone? I never ask anyone to do more than he's paid for. And yet, if the man is a technician, he stands around and smokes at his bench, doing as little as possible and ignoring his ashtray. If he's an engineer, he is unnecessarily careless with expensive equipment. The physicists think they can get out of bed any time after eleven. I never ask anyone to do anything unreasonable. I never expect anything from a man except what I'm paying him for, but I don't get even that. Why is it so universally, unexplainably true? Why doesn't anybody want to do his job?"

My father and Dr. Sandeman, though each was tired and under some strain of disappointment, spoke to each other with sentiment about their Berkeley friends in common. Although I listened for it carefully, the laundry sack was not mentioned. Their conversation was filled with pauses, and while it may have been that these pauses were like those articulate ones which fall between people whose thoughts outstrip their words, it is certainly true that a range of taboo subjects would have existed for each on that evening. At Maryann's marriage celebration, my father would not wish to entertain the personal reminiscences he and Sandeman might have shared at another time, reminiscences which might risk comparison of his early, good work at Los Alamos, which Maryann seemed to have inspired, with his less successful work of the past year. Dr. Sandeman would not want to be asked about the bomb prototype construction, nor about the final development of the implosive lenses and their fusing circuits, nor about any one of a dozen other realms of difficulty and frustration which went to make up his flux of immediate things. They talked, but they seemed to be skipping both lines and cracks, unwilling to break either a father's spine or a mother's back.

"Is it time to test it already?" began old Dr. Orr, who had joined us again, along with Richie Mundi, who was still wearing his best man's tuxedo. This was very late in the evening, and some of the guests had already departed. "Can it actually be time nearly for our test? I think we just came here," Orr said.

"There wasn't all that much to it," Richie said. "The scientist's part in the thing is nearly finished. The whole business is in the hands of the engineers and technicians now."

That was the moment when the incident in the parking lot began. We watched from a window. The two automobiles were crashing into each other, backing away, and crashing again. They chased each other around the parking lot, now getting a parked car between them and now skirting around it, one occasionally catching the other from behind. One of the cars stopped for good. The men fought on with their fists in the dirt.

"There's the fellow who knocked Sandeman's teeth out," my father said. Mal was standing just inside the door of the reception room, looking out into the parking lot. "I wonder what he's doing here."

In the card-playing room, the drinking continued. Nelse Nachtigall drank conspicuously more than the others. He seemed to be flying toward some record, some limit, and then, with very little ceremony or congratulation, he passed it.

"That's it," he said. "The vowels make a song."

204

"What?" everyone asked.

"The vowels are a song. Terrific! Listen to this:

> *A.E., I.O.U.,*
> *Albert Einstein, I.O.U.,*
> *For all my modern physics can do . . ."*

He sang the words to a melody he had presumably also made up. But he stopped abruptly. Everyone waited for him to continue.

"Go on," people said.

"I can't," he said. "I can't find a place for my word, 'supple.' It won't go in the song."

"Look, these kids aren't interested in playing cards," Richie said to my father. "Why don't you take them for a swim?" He was talking about the swimming pool and steam baths in another part of the hotel. They were rarely used, except by people from the East.

"Or, for that matter, you could," my father said. He doesn't swim, and he may not have felt like wading at that particular moment.

"I'll take them," Selina Meisner said. She pushed her chair away from the coffee table where Dr. Orr was cutting the cards.

"Oh, don't be silly," Richie said. "I'll take them. It isn't any trouble."

"Dance?" Dr. Nachtigall asked. "Let's do the supple. Come on, Selina, supple with me."

"It isn't any trouble for me, either," Selina said. "I feel like swimming. And you may all have some gossip to spread about me anyway." She smiled, but whatever she had wanted to work hadn't worked. Selina's English pronunciation was much better than that of Orr or Ferrini, but her ease with colloquial idioms was not yet complete. For example, she might come to a card table where a poker game was in progress and ask, "Mind if I sit down on your hand?" And the lechers would smile at each other.

It was decided that Selina would take us swimming. "Be good girls, now, and don't give Dr. Meisner any trouble," Colonel DiCicco told his daughters. I said I didn't want to go because I hadn't brought my bathing suit.

"They have bathing suits at the pool," Richie said.

"Does he need any money?" my father asked at large.

"They put it on our bill for us," Richie said. "The Army pays."

"Nice of them," my father said, putting his wallet away.

"How about renting a room upstairs," Dr. Nachtigall suggested. "We could all rent a room upstairs and go up there and supple."

We followed Selina out of the card room up a short flight of stairs into the main lobby. Selina timidly asked someone where the pool was. We went through a door and found ourselves walking over a bricked floor.

At the pool entrance, we found bathing suits hanging up and went into separate locker rooms to put them on. When I joined them by the side of the pool, I was surprised to see how much the ladies' bathing suits looked like my own. The ladies' suits were two-piece, a dark blue color with white stitching. The bra part was reasonably brief and had white buttons terminating the straps.

Selina was an excellent swimmer. She dove in and swam two lengths of the pool without even warming up. We had all heard how German girls were brought up in the tradition of athletics and how they craved exercise, but here Selina was proving it for us. After her first two lengths, she climbed out and dried herself off.

"It's fun," she said. "Get in."

Daisy had already dunked herself at the low end of the pool and was now doing dives from the high board. Eunice and I still hadn't been in. The underwater lights beneath the surface looked like luminous holes through which the pool manager might be planning to let glowing, poisonous eels once we were all in. The black lines marking the lane boundaries on the bottom sustained this impression, for what did they look like by the time they reached the surface but undulating snakes? Splash! Daisy dove between two snakes and rudely parted them.

Selina dove in again and swam six lengths at a fast crawl without stopping. By the middle of her marathon, both Eunice and I were in, but we didn't do much except dog-paddle from one handgrip on the pool wall to another. I would not have been so lazy if my mother had been there watching: she would have complained that all my swimming lessons at home had gone for nothing.

"Dr. Meisner!" Daisy called out when Selina surfaced after her last lap. "How about a race?"

Selina was still breathing hard. "Yes!" she called back. "What's your pleasure?" The funny acoustics of the water surface and the tiled walls made Selina's voice come from every corner of the pool except where she really was. I was trying to put my foot over one of the underwater lights to see if it was warm. It wasn't.

"Four laps," Daisy said, padding over the tiles in wet feet to the rim above our heads. "Free style."

Selina lifted herself out of the water and took her place

beside Daisy. They positioned themselves by stretching out their arms until their fingers no longer touched. Daisy counted three and they were off, tearing up the water like stern-wheelers. Daisy took a large initial lead in the first half-lap, presumably because she was rested, but Selina began challenging her by the time they turned around for the second lap. Selina took over the lead at the third turn, possibly because of the adroitness of her turn, but Daisy was red-hot during the last lap and the two reached the final wall almost simultaneously. If there had been a photographer, he probably would have pronounced Daisy the winner, but it would have required at least photographic evidence to prove this.

Selina boosted herself out of the pool and dried herself with a towel. She used a separate towel on her hair, rubbing her scalp briskly. "I'll leave you now," she said. "Daisy, you'll take care of the smaller ones? You're a better swimmer than I anyway." She walked out of the pool room hiking up her swim suit which had slipped at her waist. The suit had been made to accommodate a larger pair of hips. Our last sight of Selina, smoothing back her wet blond mane, was regal, serene.

Daisy and Eunice dawdled in the water. I watched the electric clock above the entrance to the steam rooms count off half an hour. The two girls chased each other off the diving board and generally engaged in activity which excluded me. Then Daisy got out of the water and wandered off into the steam rooms, leaving Eunice and me alone in the pool. We swam independently, and I practiced my frog kick. We heard a shower running in the steam room.

"I'm going with Daisy," Eunice said, and left me. It seemed like a poor risk to stay in the pool alone, so I followed her.

The interior of the steam room was only moderately lit: it would have been intensely bright had it not been filled with heavy, hot water vapor. Eunice and I felt a warm shock in our lungs with the first breaths we took of the humid air. It was like having someone breathe on you from the inside. Daisy didn't seem to be there immediately, but soon we saw her faintly through the clouds, sitting on the tiled floor leaning against the tiled wall. We walked closer. Even as we came close to her, the milky steam made Daisy ghostlike. Her hair had extremely tiny droplets in it everywhere. They shone and reflected light in that special way eyes do in a room with a naked bulb.

Daisy reached up and took my hand. Water showers were everywhere in the room, and I was standing in one. The shower was warm and it pounded my shoulders and my back. Daisy held my hand, but it felt as if the shower were holding me all over. It was really quite impossible to see an arm's length away. Eunice was nowhere in sight. It was just Daisy and me, and Daisy drew me down beside her. She kissed me. Her breasts touched my chin with their blue tightness. They were stitch-stitched all over and blue and wet. Daisy's eyes were on me. She touched me in a very sensitive spot, and that spot enlarged and hardened. She placed my hand on her bra. She unfastened herself behind, and the shoulder straps came down, and a wonderful falling thing happened until we were very close. I was amazed how they felt. I had once asked a friend who had a steady girl how they felt, and he had said terrific, but I had never thought this terrific. Not particularly hard, or firm, like they look in magazines. On Daisy's mute suggestion, I lay on my back and she lowered herself toward me. She dragged the very tip-ends gently across my chest. Her neck was up, her face lost in a cloud of steam. An unbelievable feeling. Daisy came down, and we lay side by side on the tile letting the bright, cloudy rain fall on us. Daisy's hand on my swim suit felt like an extension of the rain. Untied. Then totally freed. Daisy's hands. Never had this brick-hard feeling before. Something unbelievable about to happen. Daisy still with her bottom on. Breasts on me, touching me there. Should wait. Should. Can't.

Daisy backing away. Fountain. Is she watching? Yes. Is it over? No. No. Yes. Daisy lay beside me again. Over. She didn't want it from me. Only wanted to look? Nipples touching my cheek. We stop and let my heart go whack, whack.

"The blueing didn't do anything to me?"

Daisy raised her head and looked at me, her expression a question.

"From before," I whispered. "From the time we were together before." Daisy's arm still across my chest.

"As far as I can tell, no."

"I was afraid my balls were blued forever," I said.

The showers in the steam room rattle down on us. My tears made invisible by them.

"They're not," she said.

chapter twenty-four

I HAVE ASKED MY FATHER to set problems for me to do in the evening hours I find myself awake and in need of entertainment. He does this, but both of his favorite styles of problem are unsatisfying, ultimately. The first type, problems he invents for me to do out of his own head, are always too simple in their fundamental conception and requirement of basic understanding: they seem to be exercises in algebraic manipulation, as if this were all he thought his son could really do. On the other hand, the problems he sets for me out of my own textbooks, while subtle and challenging, are likely to be ones I have worked before, and therefore more concerned with the process of remembering than of discovering.

What concerns me most about this apparent failure of my father to propose the problems I imagine could really satisfy me is that I am not too stupid to see this as an allegory of my greater relationship to research physics. The problems he writes out are straightforward in principle but tedious in detail, as if they were too recently part of some stream of practical questions looking for practical answers. But the questions I like to hear are the ones proposed in terms so mathematical, so powerful, so general, the scientific questions which are so classical that they tend already to have answers. The one alternative is tedium, the other is nostalgia, and the middle ground is obscured.

"Who set the problems for each of you during the war, at Los Alamos?" I asked my father recently.

"In one sense," he said, "they were set for us by Frisky Sandeman and the Division Heads, Ferrini and Orr. But I think that this couldn't have worked unless we also set them for ourselves."

"You took something up and worked on it until you got tired of it? Or until you found the answer? Until when?"

"It's probably fair to say that we changed our own research objectives weekly. You know that we met Tuesday afternoons in a somewhat formal seminar session where a different man each week would present his research for public inspection. After the lecture, the discussion would usually become a general forum for any of the projects under way. This was a pretty difficult place to back a bad idea, and many ideas died there."

"I understand that Dr. Meisner once proposed that the atomic bomb was going to blow up the earth at one of these meetings."

"That's right, she did. I don't remember much about it, except that she frightened a lot of people. She wrote some excellent calculations on the blackboard which made it look as though we were frigging around with the end of the world. But I think Sandeman and Ferrini talked her out of it."

Selina stands away from the blackboard, her back to her audience. The air is dark with what, smoke? Chalk dust? No one speaks; every eye is on Selina's calculations. Blond mane, yellow suit, the fingers of her left hand touching her chin. No sound. The numbers on the blackboard say that uranium fission temperatures could ignite a nuclear fusion reaction in the atmosphere. Nothing less than this. The bomb could light the air.

"How did they talk her out of it?" I asked my father.

"This was so long ago, fifteen years, isn't it? I can't remember the detail, but Sandeman made an issue of one of her assumptions. He and Ferrini had done this calculation before. They said they hadn't been able really to convince themselves that ignition of the atmosphere was impossible, but they believed it was remote. Those of us who heard the argument were troubled that there wasn't much to choose between Selina's assumptions and Sandeman's: they were both idealizing a very complicated problem. Then Zimas brought up the possibility of actually trying for a thermonuclear reaction by packing an atomic bomb in liquid deuterium. Ferrini said they had also thought of this and were convinced it was within the realm of possibility. He said they had been planning to hide the idea and think about it themselves, but the younger people kept reinventing it.

The argument raging, Sandeman and the others at the blackboard with chalk in their hands. Selina standing to one side, passed by the emotional rush. People doing their own independent calculations on the backs of envelopes, corners of the blackboard. Selina drinking coffee, talking to Nelse Nachtigall. No one can be heard.

"You touch on something here," I said to my father, "which I desperately want to know. I looked for it in school, but never found it. I expected to find it in my job, but the people there didn't know what it was. It's what I want you to lead me to in my problems, but you can't, you won't, or at least you never do. It's what Selina did by herself, but it was nothing until you all did it together."

"I think you understand this somewhat wrong," my father said.

"That's possible," I said. "And it's also possible you aren't giving your full attention to what I'm saying. I'm telling you that I see you standing among all these people at Selina's seminar. You're settling yourselves in the happy bloom of adventure in science, with all your training and talent intact and together for the first time. Selina is still young and pretty. You're inventing things, flying. And I'm frightened because I know this will never happen to me."

"What makes you so sure it won't happen to you?"

I seem to be standing by the mountain brook. In Maryann's hand appear to be dead testicles, bleeding blue, dead blood into the water.

"My own fears," I said.

"Well, I can hardly reply to that," my father said. "I don't know what your fears are. You won't tell anybody."

"Some time I will," I said. "Some time I'll tell you all of it."

214

chapter twenty-five

Mrs. Mundi appeared to be getting better a month or so after Maryann's wedding, but that turned out to be an illusion. Her husband drove to Albuquerque often to see her, and his friends were only too happy to help by supplying him with their gasoline and tire ration coupons. Dr. Mundi spent many of his lonely evenings repairing and modifying a set of military two-way radios, but the federal security men came and confiscated them before he could take the one he had built for Gloria to her in the hospital. It was unlikely that Gloria's voice could be heard over a two-way radio by that time anyway. The Mundis continued to play their game of tearing up their letters before they put them in envelopes, but now the puzzles came through already solved.

One afternoon during this time my father and I accompanied Dr. Mundi on one of his visits to Gloria. The tires on his old car were bald, and it was impossible to get new ones, so when we had our first flat, we had to find another tire as well as tube. All this happened on the highway. We were hours late getting to the hospital, and the visiting period was nearly over. Gloria was at this time feeling a great deal of pain. She was nearly unconscious throughout our stay, which lasted only a few minutes. Her whiteness, the slimness of her neck, and the puff of the feather bedding drawn over her breasts are the images I see when I remember this, our last visit with her.

She lay very still on her bed. One had the feeling that although her eyes were closed and she appeared to dream, she was quite aware of us, quite sure of who we were, comprehending of our relative permanence and her transience, and so it must have been a bit of wit, what she said, when the door drifted open behind us and Richie reached over and closed it: "Who went out?"

I was going to school during the day, and therefore unable to leave the mesa very often, even though my father was now traveling to the desert test site nearly every day. Only once was I permitted to skip school and ride out to the desert with my father, and that turned out to be at the special invitation of Dr. Sandeman. My father explained this to me before we left the mesa. Dr. Sandeman was interested in having his laundry bag back, at the latest by this very evening. I wasn't to say anything about this to anyone. My father and I were to ride to the base camp together, but from there Dr. Sandeman would take me alone out to the place where my father and I had left the laundry bag. Sandeman had taken my father out there on searches for the laundry bag several times earlier, with no success. Perhaps I could recognize the terrain. It had been eight months since my father and I had been responsible for its loss, but it sounded to me as if, for some unstated reason, this would be the last chance we would have to look for it.

The base camp looked how to me? Unimaginable, I should say. Twenty miles of new blacktop road had been built since I had last been here. At the end of this road there rose before us as we drove up a complete scientific laboratory in the desert. Lines of portable CCC structures made the place look like a city. As we waited for Sandeman to come and pick me up, my father pointed out at least three barracks, a service-and-supply building, a quartermaster office, repair shops, warehouses, a mess hall and kitchen, and a building for offices, laboratories, and officers' quarters. As at Los Alamos, vehicles were perpetually moving in the streets between the buildings: trucks, bulldozers, modified weapons carriers, automobiles.

"The yard where the bulldozers are parked is a snake nest in the mornings," my father said. "Each morning the drivers have to pound wrenches on their bulldozers to get the rattlesnakes out."

My father showed me two specially modified Sherman tanks which he explained had two-inch-thick lead walls. The tanks were completely sealed, and carried oxygen bottles inside to sustain the operators. One of the tanks had a picture painted on the side, of a woman riding a bicycle with no shirt on, only a blue woolen cap on her head, with the words, "Ferrini's Phaeton" lettered below.

Dr. Sandeman picked me up driving his own jeep. It had a canvas top, and may have been the only vehicle I saw that day with the doors still on it. The interior reeked of stale cigarettes. Dr. Sandeman smoked as he drove me northward into the desert. Did I smoke yet? he asked me. No, I said. How old was I now? Fifteen, I answered. He could remember me much younger, he told me. At my direction he turned off the access road northeast toward Compania Hill.

The desert roughness seemed impossibly strange from the inside of our smoky box. Dr. Sandeman's hand on the gear shift seemed to be squeezing yellowness out of the cigarette into the skin of the two fingers being used for a cigarette holder. Driving along like that, roughly, being bounced hard into the sides of the vehicle, it was difficult to look carefully at Dr. Sandeman. I often found it hard to see for myself the intellectual sex appeal everybody said he had. Today he was wearing neither his work shirt, nor his jeans, nor his wide belt with the silver buckle: today he had on a business suit and a wide tie. The porkpie hat was lying in the back among rattling gasoline jerry cans. Dr. Sandeman used the back of his hand to wipe the windshield, but it did no good, the pale dust was there on the outside. I asked him to stop when I thought we were near the place my father and I had abandoned the laundry bag. He got out and urinated loudly on the cracking desert floor. Our dust cloud, following us, stood out behind like a still, dirty contrail.

Dr. Sandeman asked me a strange question. "What do you think about your father?"

"What do you mean, 'What do I think about him?'"

"I mean, what have you noticed about him?"

Dr. Sandeman had blue eyes, I knew that now. He sat on one of the jeep's fenders, but he didn't take his eyes off me. He shook his cigarette package until one of his cigarettes fell into the dust, but he picked this up, flicked it off, and lit it anyway.

"I notice he's sad," I said.

"He's sad," Dr. Sandeman said. "Yes."

I looked out on the bleak desert floor and it seemed to me

218

that this could easily be the exact spot where we had been standing when Rasputin's jeep had come whirring out of the horizon. I wanted to find the bag and get back to my father.

"How else has he been recently? Irrational? Hard to live with?" Dr. Sandeman asked.

I had to admit to myself that this was beginning to become my father's reputation. I had been with him once when he had found Ferrini's bicycle parked in the space reserved for our truck next to the laboratories. He had picked it up and thrown it out of the way. Ferrini, seeing him do this, had come out and wanted to fight about it.

"What do you think it's all about?" Sandeman asked at last.

"I think it's about Maryann," I said. I wasn't sure just how much Sandeman knew about Maryann and her relationship with my father and me. Just who is privileged to common knowledge? How high does it go?

"You think he's disappointed because Maryann has left him and married Nelse Nachtigall?"

"Yes," I said.

"And that's all," Sandeman said.

"Yes," I said. It seemed like enough to me. We had already heard that Maryann was treating even her marriage rather informally, and was in the habit of being absent for days at a time.

"I see that your father is threatened," Sandeman said. "I see that he's very deeply troubled, but I also see something which perhaps you can't, namely that it all shows in his work. He can't do what he's already proved he's able to do. And I don't like it."

I was beginning to feel angry. I wondered what Sandeman thought I could do about bringing Maryann back to my father. Her dying cactus plants on the windowsill of our cabin hadn't brought her back. Nor had the fact that I had worn my lucky socks a great length of time until my father had made me change them. The still, bleak flatness of the desert stretched out in all directions away from where we stood. Low red flowers of the type Dr. Orr had pulled up on our picnic day almost two years ago pattered on the ground around the jeep's wheels. That day, Maryann's dancing had kicked up the dusty desert, and the silt which was just now coming to earth seemed to be the very last of Maryann's motion. Her dance with us had started on a spring morning in Tennessee, and we had, all three of us, traced it on a road map across the highways to Santa Fe, and then through the brilliance of air-dried cactus and pine to Los Alamos. Maryann danced for us, although she said she was dancing for herself.

"I must admit I have a different impression about why your father is sad," Sandeman said. "I think he's sad about you."

My blood jumped. I felt an enormous sense of panic.

"I'd like to tell you about your father," Sandeman said, nearly whispering. "I wonder if you'll understand me." Sandeman was silent for a moment, perhaps thinking about what he wanted to say to me. "Damn the war," Sandeman said, sort of to himself. "If I had more than ten minutes, I might be able to keep this from sounding so arbitrary. Maybe when you think of this later, you'll keep in mind how much I regard you and your father, how I want to help you, and how little time I have."

"I wish you'd say why I'm making my father sad," I said.

Sandeman seemed unwilling to leave the ferry docks of San Francisco, or wherever his imagination had carried him searching for his old friendship with my father, but he replied finally, "I think he's unhappy because he sees his son, whom he loves, acting vitiated and weak, and somehow blaming him."

"Weak," I repeated.

"Yes," Sandeman said. I considered where I had heard this before. Mrs. Wulfkopf, my teacher in the Army school at Los Alamos, had implied something like this. Others also: Daisy. But what kind of strength was one supposed to have? And when he has it, how does he show it? A bone-crushing handshake? Publicly attended feats of strength? Surely the calisthenics in front of a mirror Mrs. Wulfkopf had in mind were supposed to be done in private.

"I wish I understood what you were talking about," I said.

"I'm talking about what's bothering you," Sandeman said. "I want to talk about what's bothering you. You're taciturn and withdrawn. You seem unwilling to share a friendship, or for that matter, any relationship with anyone at all, at least anyone I know. You act as if your balls had grown in the size of blueberries, and it's making your father damned miserable."

Blueberries. Really quite an image. I thought about blueberries. My parents and I picked them on walking trips in New Hampshire. In Tennessee, the fields seen from the windows of our truck had blueberries in them. I felt unable to breathe, as if Richie Mundi's odor amplifier had concentrated the smell of the world's wealth of blueberries under my nose.

"Remember I say this because I need your father and he needs you," Sandeman said.

The sun dwelt above us brilliantly, looking for the laundry bag along with us. In places where there were creosote bushes, the sharp shadows from which the bushes seemed to grow were pushed into great drifts which blew in the slightest breeze.

"It's a bad thing," Sandeman said, "experiencing the kind of crisis you seem to be having. I've had them myself and I know they're painful. I wish you could trust me to know whatever it is that makes you so unhappy. You'd do yourself an enormous favor in confiding it to someone. You make a mistake in feeling that you're alone." I wanted to believe him.

When we arrived back at base camp later that afternoon, I felt Dr. Sandeman and I had somehow used this occasion to become friends. My father picked me up at Sandeman's office and brought me to the assembly laboratory where he was working with Richie Mundi and Nelson Nachtigall.

chapter twenty-six

THE LABORATORY MY FATHER, NELSE AND RICHIE shared at
the base camp was much smaller than their equivalent one at
Los Alamos. The building was one of those temporary wooden
structures one saw everywhere, both on the mesa and now
here on the desert. A single glass skylight was fitted in the
roof above our heads, but now that the sun was setting, this
provided very little light, and in fact the fluorescent lamp had
already been turned on by the time my father brought me into
the room. An uninitiated person might have mistaken the red,
glowing skylight above the gas bottles, copper tubing, and
electronics support equipment to be part of someone's
experiment. There were handwritten signs in several places
warning of the danger due to high voltage. The ever-present
blackboard with circuit diagrams on it occupied one narrow
wall.

"I asked him, Harold," Richie said, as soon as we entered
the room. "I asked him and he said no."

"How much time did you ask him for?" my father said.

"Five hours," Richie replied. "I don't see how I could drive to Albuquerque and back and still have any time with Gloria in less than five hours."

My father looked at his watch. "He must still be planning it for dawn tomorrow. I don't think it's going to be tomorrow, though. We've got a thunderstorm alert for about that time."

"I was thinking of going anyway," Dr. Mundi said.

"Well," my father said, and then nothing more. It wasn't a very positive reply.

"If the shot doesn't go, it's not very likely I'll be missed," Dr. Mundi said. "If I leave now, I'm sure I can be back before two or two thirty."

"Who would arm your cameras?" my father asked.

"I armed them already," Dr. Mundi said. He seemed to be putting down his screwdriver and taking off his lab coat. He seemed to be getting ready to leave.

"So you're going, then," my father said.

"I think so, Harold."

"Well," my father said.

"Well, yourself," replied Dr. Mundi. He put on his jacket.

"You'll be back at two?"

"I'll do the best I can," he said, and walked out the door.

Nelse Nachtigall looked up from his experimental apparatus and watched Dr. Mundi leave.

"He's been useless in here all day," Dr. Nachtigall said. "I don't see why Sandeman told him he couldn't see his wife. Maybe when he gets back, he'll pay a little more attention to what he's doing. Did you see this over here?" Dr. Nachtigall pointed to the edge of Mundi's steel workbench, which had a metal belt buckle welded to it. "That was a bad accident."

"How did he do that?" my father asked.

224

"I don't know how he did it," Dr. Nachtigall said. "I came in this afternoon and there it was. He told me he accidentally grounded something through his belt buckle as he was leaning over his bench."

"He didn't hurt himself?" my father asked.

"No, he didn't hurt himself," Dr. Nachtigall said. "He never hurts himself. It's a miracle." Nachtigall was making banana plug leads with a pair of wire strippers and a screwdriver. He was using a soldering iron. When my father left us alone for a few minutes, I told him something.

"Two of Maryann's cactus plants have died, but one of the little ones looks like it's going to be all right."

Dr. Nachtigall looked kind of hurt. He put down his tools and sat on a chair.

"Would you like me to tell her that?" he asked.

"Yes," I said. "I think I was watering them too much. It's funny how I found out. I got sick of taking care of them, and I was going to let them all die, so I stopped watering them. But that made some of them better."

"Wouldn't you rather tell her yourself?"

"I hardly ever see her," I said.

"Well, just now I don't see so much of her either," Dr. Nachtigall said. "But if I do see her, I'll tell her."

I had many questions I wanted to ask Dr. Nachtigall about Maryann, but just then I decided to take it easy on him. "If I see her first, I'll tell her," I said.

"O.K.," he said. "Whoever sees her first will tell her."

The sun finished going down and the red skylight in the roof of the laboratory became black. Dr. Nachtigall and my father loaded some electronic equipment into a jeep waiting outside the building. The thunderstorms forecast for morning were still not yet in evidence in the sky. Instead, there were stars as high as one wanted to look, and only a few mackerel clouds around the moon. I was reminded of clear nights like this on our trip to the West, when Maryann and my father and I would stop, long after midnight, and enjoy the pointedness of the stars before going to bed.

When the equipment was loaded, Dr. Nachtigall drove down the access road toward ground zero in the moonlit desert. My father and I returned to the laboratory. I helped in the calibration of a clock device by turning a switch on and off when my father told me to. The laboratory building seemed deserted except for us. Occasionally a vehicle would speed by on the access road, and once I heard voices walking by an open window. My father smoked. He made notes in brown-covered bound notebooks. We were very much absorbed in these calibration experiments when, about ten P.M., a military policeman came in and spoke to us.

"I want to talk to a scientist named Nachtigall," he said. My father told him that Dr. Nachtigall could not be reached.

"It's about his wife," the policeman said. "I don't usually get involved in things my people do on their own time, but I think someone has to be responsible here. I want this Nachtigall to come and get his wife."

My father asked the military policeman if Maryann was all right. He made the mistake of addressing the man as "officer."

"Lieutenant," the policeman said. "She hasn't been in an accident, or anything like that, if that's what you mean. I'd rather speak to this man Nachtigall."

My father turned off the clock calibration equipment. He led the policeman to a lounge room where there were chairs and magazines. "We'll be back here with Dr. Nachtigall in less than an hour," he said.

"I don't usually get involved in what goes on with my people after hours, if you know what I mean," the lieutenant said. "I'm here on my own time now."

"We'll hurry," my father promised him.

Outside, the moon was being titillated by more and more high clouds. My father seemed very serious and preoccupied. As we drove out the access road in my father's four-wheel-drive truck, I saw a package of Kleenex in the glove box. Was it Maryann's, left over from an entirely different set of times? My father drove very fast. We raced past the place where Dr. Sandeman and I had turned off into the desert. I thought about Sandeman. I wondered if there would ever be a time when I would feel like offering him my confidence, and if that time should come, if he would still want to accept it.

Lights appeared in the dark grounds before us. We drove into a scene of floodlights and milling people whose activity was full of the sense of emergency one sees in a newspaper photograph of a disaster scene. Men and equipment were everywhere, and wires led into the dark desert in every direction. A pile of lumber pointed sharp-looking slivers into our headlights, and behind this lumber, incredibly, rose the four wide-apart base supports of a high steel tower. My father parked the truck near a mass of other vehicles. Selina Meisner spoke to us as we got out.

"Harold, will you please help me?" she asked. My father helped her move a heavy piece of electronic equipment from a truck bed to the ground.

"Is this plug supposed to go into four hundred cycles?" she asked, showing my father the plug on her electronic box. My father examined the plug. "It is, isn't it?" she demanded.

"Yes, I'm afraid it is," my father said.

"Oh, no, no, no," she wailed. "I wish I hadn't brought this

227

one. Where am I ever going to get four hundred cycles around here?"

My father asked several people where Dr. Nachtigall was, and each one replied he hadn't seen him. I remember seeing Dr. Sandeman standing in the beam of a floodlight, directing the unloading of a large crate from a flatbed truck. His hunting knife hung by his side, tied with a leather thong. He was wearing his faded blue jeans and the silver belt and pork-pie hat. The pitch his temper had reached defies description. A Negro laborer carrying a plank bumped him slightly in passing. Sandeman shoved him back, and the man fell heavily in the dirt.

"I'm sorry," Sandeman said, picking the man up. "I'm so sorry. I lost my temper. I've lost my temper so often tonight. It's this job, this inhuman job. I'd gladly give it to you, if you'd take it. I have the whole responsibility for the success of this project. I'm the leader, yet they question me at every turning. They never leave me alone, and Ornberg at the Radiation Lab on the Coast takes all the money and wastes it while nobody says anything. I'd gladly trade jobs with you. Come on, you be me."

The black man listened with round eyes. He looked at Sandeman's hand clutching his arm. Sandeman's voice was loud and shrill. The tense moment ended when Sandeman was called to the radiotelephone set. We continued to look for Dr. Nachtigall. It was finally Selina Meisner who told us she thought he was up in the tower.

How did we climb the tower? There were no stairs. My father and I rode to the top in the wooden cage of an improvised elevator. Through the chain link door of the elevator cage we saw the steel struts and stays of the tower moving down, occa-

228

sionally reflecting the lights of the scene below. An aircraft obstruction light midway up gleamed into the cage. We heard the sound of the winch above us coming closer and closer until we emerged through a hole in the upper platform and stepped out. An iron shed occupied nearly the whole of this upper floor. We entered the shed through a narrow door and there I saw it. Black, spherical, with heavy cables sticking into it from all directions, the bomb was bolted down on an oak floor.

There was no one present in the shed whom I recognized. We asked a guard if he had seen Dr. Nachtigall, but the man couldn't help us. We had a last look from face to face among the people there before taking the elevator to the ground. After looking for and asking after Dr. Nachtigall for over half an hour, my father and I agreed that it was possible he had somehow eluded us and returned to the base camp. We found our truck among the maze of vehicles and drove back the way we had come.

Colonel DiCicco and his daughter Daisy were waiting for us when we arrived.

"Are you going out to the tower?" Colonel DiCicco asked my father. "I'd like to ride with you. We're here on my daughter's motorcycle. I don't want to drive it out there."

My father told Colonel DiCicco that we were driving in the other direction. He seemed very disappointed. We picked up the military policeman and left a note for Dr. Nachtigall on his desk:

COME IMMEDIATELY TO POPE
R.R. SIDING, M.P. BARRACKS
— H.

229

I caught sight of Daisy sitting on her motorcycle in the darkness outside before we left. She was smoking a cigarette, and her feet were curled up underneath her. She returned my wave.

The military policeman led the way in his jeep and we followed in our truck. Vaporous shadows often darkened his taillights in front of us, shadows which might have been caused either by dust raised from the desert floor or the thicker clouds now floating across the moon. Cattle fences rippled off to one side, and once a cattle guard clattered under our wheels. Where we crossed the Rio Grande, the moon suddenly became bright and made the cliffs around the river gulch sharp and white.

"If I see Maryann, I'm going to tell her that Mrs. Woods is pregnant and they think she's going to have twins," I told my father.

"What?" my father asked. "Why should you want to tell her that?"

"Because she was wrong," I said. A bright momentary hole of moonlight reflected in the white Army star painted on our hood.

"She was wrong," my father repeated, trying to remember. Then he did remember. "Oh, yes," he said. "She used to say suspicious things about Frank Woods. She thought he was incapable of children. But I didn't know you were aware of this. You want her to take it back, do you?"

"Yes," I said.

My father looked over at me. Did he care that Maryann had been proven wrong? He looked back at the road.

"You want to have some victory over her?"

"We don't need her," I said. "She was wrong about a lot of things."

"She was wrong to think we didn't love her, wouldn't you say?" my father asked me. "That's the only mistake she ever made I care about." A pause, then, "You'll have your victory over her tonight. I have a feeling she needs us very badly. She's drowning."

My father's image extended itself through the windshield into the underwater contrasts of the moonlit gulches and cliffs outside, which were already dimming again under the marches of clouds.

"Maryann's sister drowned," I said.

"And now she's drowning, herself," my father replied.

Our road brought us up and down over dim little hills, unusual in New Mexico, a consequence of the nearness of the Rio Grande. I knew that even from the top of one of these hills I would never be able to see the Albuquerque hospital where Gloria was dying, or even the military police barracks ahead where my father thought Maryann needed us. It was certainly absurd to think that I saw the laundry bag, which must now have been fifty miles distant, but I saw it anyway, a bright white point on our left in the desert. I asked my father to stop the truck. I told him what I saw.

"I'd rather believe you could see into the future," he said, "than believe you could see Sandeman's laundry bag from here. Forget that thing forever," my father said, and even as he did, the desert paled and I lost sight of my white point.

"You and I can forget it, even if Sandeman can't," he went on. "The Feds will find it for him. They really will. Some time ten years from now, the Feds will dredge that thing up and bring it back to him. And then he'll have his bag of ten-year-old dirty laundry back. Won't that be swell?"

The military policeman led us down a long, sloping road in the foothills of the Fra Cristobal mountains. The foothills themselves, bald and craggy, climbed up all around us as we pointed our headlights at them. A few piñon pines, low and trashy, were the only trees that stood out when our headlights stretched into the darkness of the bending road. The military policeman's taillamps got closer to us: he was slowing down. I saw the Pope railroad siding and the military police barracks, and then we stopped under dirty windows with lights shining through them.

"Are you going to bring your kid inside?" the lieutenant asked my father.

"He's not allowed?" my father said.

"He's allowed if you allow him," the lieutenant said, "but I wouldn't bring my kid in to watch it."

My father asked me to stay outside. The lieutenant wanted to know one thing more. "Are you going to take her out with you?"

"You'd prefer that?" my father asked.

"I want someone to get her out," the lieutenant said.

"I'll bring her out if she wants to come," my father answered. The lieutenant and my father left and walked around to the front of the building, where the door was. Besides the cooling, clinking sounds of our truck's engine, there was nothing but a bad silence. A bit of night wind frothed the desert dust beyond the barracks. It blew dirt into the low, garbagey piñons. By climbing on the hood of the truck, I could see inside through a dirty window.

I saw my father and the lieutenant standing in the doorway. I saw many men standing around, perhaps ten. And Maryann was there, lying on a bottom bunk. Her skin was wet, on a hot night, wet with sweat? No, worse. No one moved toward her at first, while my father was standing there. But then Mal tried to touch her, and she wouldn't let him.

My father came to her. They spoke. Nothing moved, none of the people there. No one even listening, no one willing to overhear. Then I remember Maryann's dark arms reaching up, my father bending, kissing her goodbye. Holding her hand one moment more. And then turning, leaving. The others standing motionless, strangers, thinking about how they will go again into, into her.

chapter twenty-seven

I HAVE JUST ARISEN from the most remarkable dream, Mary-ann, whose details I feel I must tell you, but I have a certain apprehension. You know how unusual it is for me to remember my dreams; I can recall your having said something to my father once: "How odd, Timmy doesn't remember his dreams." And this hasn't changed. I suppose there isn't any real reason why such a feature so personal should change as one grows older. But tonight (it's very late evening, I find myself now wearing all my clothes, having fallen asleep that way on my bed) I remember my dream. Moments ago, lying in the darkness which extends out of my room and all over the house, as I pretended to tell you my dream, I was afraid you might interrupt to say you knew it already.

I am probably awake now because of my irritating sunburn. There seems to be no way for me to avoid accumulating another raw layer of it every day I work on the barn. This is a problem you never seemed to have had much trouble with at

Los Alamos, although many of the Easterners did. Unlike many of us, you could be brown and careless about exposure to the sun from the early weeks of summer. The habits we had together in those days are with me even now. Sometimes I trace my day as if I were with you. "Now she's eating breakfast," I say, eating alone. "Now she's at work," I say later, getting my painting supplies together. The view from my ladder of the flat fields of Dover reminds me somewhat of looking down on the desert from the mesa.

In my dream, Daisy and I were looking for you on Daisy's motorcycle. We had a conspiracy to find you and save you, since this was the night of the test and we believed that you were wandering on the desert with the wish to lose yourself and die. Daisy's motorcycle was very real: I held Daisy's waist and the motorcycle breathed hot air on my legs while Daisy's tears blew back into my eyes. We found no one in the military police barracks and started up the Fra Cristobal road. An ice storm midway up the mountain made our cheeks sting and reflected our headlight among hoary ice-covered trees. Holding Daisy so and the stimulation of our motion caused me to have a gentle, pressing erection, which I enjoyed. The road appeared uncertain before us and we stopped, but then the ice storm cleared. The moon was much nearer, larger than it is supposed to be. From our mountain vantage we watched Mr. Poupolatos land his airplane on the desert and pick you up. Even though you were far away, we could see you getting into the rear cockpit. Then Daisy and I noticed that we were really not on a mountain at all but at the top of a large tower, with a thick green carpet and an ornate balcony. There was a dumbwaiter by which a silver pitcher could be drawn up from below.

The social service person in Boston, Mr. Grey, refuses to do anything impressive in my presence; I'm beginning to think he can't impress me. In spite of the absurd postures he puts himself in when he sits in his chair, something refuses to let me be intimate with him. Every time I see him, I think to myself, "I don't remember his nostril hair being so thick," and this gets in the way of our relationship. Even so, he gets a big bang out of the stories I tell him about you and all of us in New Mexico. He's particularly interested in you.

Recently I told him about how you used to cook breakfast in the morning wearing only your nightie. You stood at the stove and turned the bacon with a fork. The sun illuminated the bows on your nightie and made you look as if you were carrying butterflies on your breasts. Nelse Nachtigall and Richie Mundi often came for breakfast, but you never wore a robe. They would stare at you, and their hands would shake as they buttered their toast. "God, you're beautiful, Maryann," Dr. Mundi would say. "You should go like that all the time. You should never wear underclothes. Just like you are now. You're one of the few women who could do it." The morning sunlight made the nightie all but transparent sometimes as you walked from the stove to the breakfast table. The tips of your breasts would often tell us that you felt the cold. You would say, "I don't know why everyone has to get so sexed up. We're all mammals, aren't we?"

Mr. Grey often asks me questions about incidents from our lives in New Mexico. "I'm curious," he said recently, "about the impression Mrs. Mundi's death seems to have made upon you. You often date things, for example, by saying whether they occurred before or after Mrs. Mundi's death. Can you think of any reason why the fact of her dying is important to you?"

He was feeling for something I also wished to touch, and I

tried to help him. "I could never understand any real reason why she had to die."

"You felt someone owed you an explanation?"

Explanation sounded like the wrong word. I tried to recall the moment when my father had told me Gloria was dead. It was some time after we returned to Boston after the war. The things he had said then had been about the lives and deaths of human beings, but I can't avoid noticing now that they also apply to the lives and deaths of ideas. Richie's odor amplifier, for example, never found an application: he reluctantly dropped interest in it after the war. Selina's dramatic prediction of the ignition of the atmosphere turned out not to be true, although if people could have been convinced that it was, atomic bombs might never have been tested. I understand, from the things my father's friends say today, that many of them believed they had found a way to work together outside of the constraints of national distinctions to make war impossible and peace bountiful. It didn't happen. The end of an idea, the proof of its fallacy, would leave people in something very much like mourning for a period, as if it were a true death. This was because everyone's heart was in the project so much that he counted his own personal fortune in the population of ideas which, taken as a whole, would say true things: in this respect it was a period of great selflessness. The death of a beautiful but impractical idea, which I gather struck the Los Alamos community as Gloria's death struck me, diminished the total hope, diminished each individual hope. My father, telling me of Gloria's death, was genuinely saddened.

Speaking of Gloria reminds me that Richie was here and spent a week with us recently. My parents monopolized most of his time in the evenings, but during the day, while my father was at work, he would help me paint the barn. Inevitably, we would talk about the days we spent together in New Mexico.

"All that is apparently over now," he told me. "After the war, none of us could pretend to be the same people we were before we went to Los Alamos. Except Ornberg, of course. He was a prick before, during, and after the war. But he was never at Los Alamos. The way the people who had been at the mesa changed: contrary to what some of my friends say, I think this has less to do with what we lost there than what we found."

"What *did* you find?" I asked him.

"We found it was just as hard to do good scientific work as ever, but making weapons like the atomic bomb was fairly easy. In the sense that you could plan to do it and then do it."

"And so how did this change you?"

"I don't think it changed all of us," he said, probably thinking about holding himself out as an exception. Then he admitted, "Maybe it did." I could tell he was uncomfortable talking this way and wanted to close the subject. "We do things for money now. We take the money knowing pretty well what the military will do with the results of our research. In order to get the money you have to change your suit a lot more often and you have to go to Washington all the time. You have to be like Ornberg. Sell yourself to the generals and that. You can't sit in your office and pick your nose any more. I don't think science attracts the same kind of people as before. Maybe there aren't any more of that kind of people. Maybe they all go and play the piano."

He smiled, but it was a vacant smile. When I looked at him,

he seemed to be gazing into a desert: his own image of the emptiness of physics as a modern thing to do. Its unconcern. Its narrow professionalism. Its spiritual poverty. "I don't mean to demoralize you," he said.

"You could hardly do that," I told him.

"It's just," he said, "that I wouldn't want you to plan your life around finding exactly the things that we found in physics as young men. You wouldn't be fair to yourself. These things may be alive in other disciplines, but not physics. Music, perhaps. Do you play anything?"

"No," I said.

He looked as if he wanted to tell me something about music. But of course, you can't. You have to sing it or play it or something.

"Do you do photography?" he asked me. "That seems to be popular with the young men in my department. Their conviction seems to be, 'I'm sure there's nothing more to life than high-energy particles, but just in case, I'd better buy a camera.' "

His fingernails were dirty. He had food stains on his clothes. Mostly he looked old to me. I wanted to get us out of the present into the past, where we would be more likely to recognize each other.

"Do you hear from anyone?" I asked him.

"I see Selina fairly often," he said. "She comes to my lab quite a lot."

"I always liked her," I said. "I've often wondered what happened to her after the war."

"You didn't hear about her little holiday from physics?"

"No," I said.

"You knew she was looking for someone to ride back with

her to New York when the test was over? She put an advertisement on the bulletin board at the Fuller Lodge."

I nodded.

"She interviewed several people. She discussed the candidates with Maryann, I believe. The one she finally accepted, on Maryann's advice, was a Jewish chemist from France. They required two weeks for their trip. In Yellowstone they camped under the stars. Across the prairies they slept together in hotels as man and wife. In Chicago they drank up the money Selina had put aside for her return passage to Europe. They experimented with drugs. At the end of their trip, their money was so low they had to pick up hitchhikers for gas. When they reached New York, they rented an apartment together on the East Side. They existed as bohemians for seven months. Selina supported them by selling the peasant blouses she had learned to make as a child. They borrowed a piano from friends leaving for Europe and he taught her to play. He enrolled in a composition class at Julliard. They talked of marriage."

"Is she still with this man?" I asked.

"No, there was only this seven months. Through a winter and spring, I think. They just figured it out for themselves that they wanted to get away from each other. The man booked on a boat for Le Havre. They talked and kissed and cried for hours on the dock at Twenty-fifth Street. Then he sailed and Selina went back to physics."

"And since then?" I asked him.

"Since then, nothing," he said. "Selina looks old. Her work isn't any good."

Dr. Mundi looked down at his hands. Ink whirls colored the skin in some places.

"What about Dr. Sandeman?" I asked. "Do you ever see him?"

"Not so much," Dr. Mundi said.

"I followed all the stories about him when he was in the news."

"You and everybody else," Dr. Mundi said. "They were miserable to him. They hurt him very, very badly. And you know, I think the thing that cut him the worst was that he was bored the whole time they were screwing him. He had to sit there in a chair in some committee room answering questions for about a year. All this time he could have spent working on something to do with physics, but he couldn't, because he had to go down there to that committee room every day and get fucked."

"You think he knew what the outcome of the hearings would be?"

"Well, once they dragged in that laundry bag of his with the letters from the Russian scientists in it, the decision was pretty much a foregone conclusion."

"I've always sensed that the other scientists on the project blamed my father for what happened to Sandeman. Don't you feel this?"

"Yes, I do," Dr. Mundi said. "I've even wondered, myself, if your father knew what he was doing when he abandoned the laundry bag out there. He presumably knew that Rasputin was passing this inquiry about information to Sandeman. Certainly he could have guessed what was in the laundry bag."

"No," I said. "That's just wrong, and I wonder that you and the others could have known my father so long and yet not known him. He didn't know what was in the laundry bag.

It was just too heavy for him. He had no reason to suspect anything was there. But what's more important about him, and I'm surprised that you don't recognize this about him, is that he's not curious enough to have looked in there. Not suspicious enough. Not even careful enough."

"I'd like to accept this point of view," Dr. Mundi said. "It's certainly consistent with many other aspects of his personality. The basis of his scientific creativity is unmistakably a kind of facility for free association. He can be entirely impulsive, as that great relationship he took up with Maryann will attest to, but he doesn't advertise this capriciousness as much as he actually lives it. I can't see him, as many of my friends do, as having consciously ruined Sandeman. He ruined him, but only with a petulant mistake."

"Of course I can't say, for a fact, what my father's intentions were at any point," I said. "But I was there with him, when he threw it away, and I'm sure he did it because the thing was simply too heavy to carry. I don't expect this to satisfy anybody, really. I suppose there will always be some suspicions."

"This, I think, is true," Dr. Mundi said. We painted in silence for a moment.

"Sandeman's ordeal may have been a large part of this change in the attitudes of physicists you were telling me about."

"Except, you know," Dr. Mundi said, "getting back to your father . . . he and I go on doing our work as if we weren't disappointed about anything. Your father especially. He seems to go on, you know, putting his work methodically forward. As if nothing were fucked up at all."

"Maybe for him things aren't fucked up."

"That's possible, I suppose," Dr. Mundi said. "But it puzzles me to see him survive so well, because it implies he couldn't have felt the real stuff when it was there before."

"It implies he couldn't have had the experiences you and the others can't forget."

"Something like that, but not exactly, because his Los Alamos work was really good. He should have felt it the way we did."

"Maybe he did," I said.

Maryann, I think of you in this stillness.

My parents have made me a gift of a lovely white flowering plant, and this sits in the darkness on my windowsill. It fills my room with an overpowering sweetness. If you were here enjoying it with me, it would remind you of so many things. Sticky red and purple low desert flowers: you pressed them in my father's scientific books. He didn't mind.

Tomorrow a girl I have grown very fond of comes to visit me. She has asked to come before, but I wanted her to wait until I had nearly finished the barn job. It stands now, out there in the darkness, nearly ready for her to see. It's an achievement. I'll be up on the ladder finishing the last strokes of the job as she appears on her bicycle at the crest of the hill by the woods, and then in a few more minutes she'll be with me. Her plan is to come all the way here on her bicycle, although I offered to drive in and pick her up. She says she wants to ride along slowly and see if there's any pot growing by the side of the road.

She likes pot quite a lot. Sometimes, when we meet in Boston after my Mass. General appointment, she's in an enthusiastic mood. I usually meet her near the Ritz, at the corner of

Arlington and Commonwealth. I can see her when she's blocks away, pedaling down Commonwealth toward me. The trucks swerve around her and I have bad moments as she's lost behind them, but then I see her again, wobbling this way, and she always makes it, she never gets hurt. As we walk her bike across Arlington Street to the Public Garden, I feel like cautioning her, but she makes the feeling ridiculous. As a matter of fact, the whole subject of caution and recklessness is something we work on all the time together, but never with words, because the words would never let us get very far into her abandoned life or my blocked one. "Oh, wow," she says when she sees the swans. I think she still steals things out of stores, although she tells me she's stopped.

My mother misunderstands this girl. She holds her somehow responsible for the prickle of imaginary pains in my groin which everybody who knows me can apparently see even though I never complain of them. Nevertheless, tomorrow she comes to be with me, and my parents know this, and as a demonstration of their goodwill, the flowering plant is here. It is a gift to us both.

You and the Los Alamos days in science are really over. Scientific work only threatens us now. It never accepts our love, the way it did then. A question which often comes to me is whether it was ever proper to feel love for science. Sometimes I am convinced that this group love of science was one of the things we were trying out at Los Alamos which didn't work. And mysteriously, this is part of my parents' reconciliation: they are together again because the other thing was, after all, transient. It didn't last. Fantastic. It seemed so real, but it escaped.

Sometimes, on their way to bed, my parents pass my room

and look in. I know this because I often wake and, feeling their presence, pretend to sleep on. I don't need to open my eyes to receive their message. It's the only one they ever have to tell me, and the only one I ever want to hear: come anything, they wish me well.